MONSTERS OF TEXAS

KEN GERHARD NICK REDFERN

Edited by Gavin Lloyd-Wilson
Typeset by Jonathan Downes,
Cover and Layout by Senor Spider for CFZ Communications
Using Microsoft Word 2000, Microsoft , Publisher 2000, Adobe Photoshop CS.

First published in Great Britain by CFZ Press

CFZ Press
Myrtle Cottage
Woolsery
Bideford
North Devon
EX39 5QR

ISBN: 978-1-905723-57-7

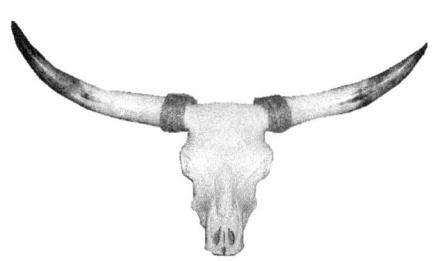

CONTENTS

Note from the authors:

The book that you now hold in your hands is very much a collaborative project; however, some of the investigations were undertaken by Ken Gerhard and others were carried out by Nick Redfern. Therefore, a number of the chapters have been written by Ken, while others were penned by Nick. In each chapter, the identity of the relevant author has been carefully identified.

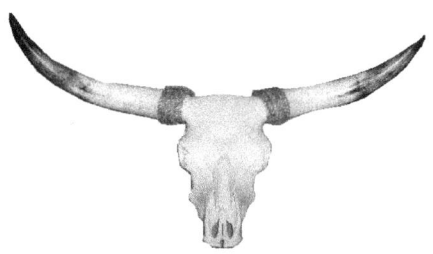

DEDICATION

For the good folk of the Lone Star State whose paths have crossed with those mysterious and monstrous beasts from beyond the veil…

Introduction

Texas – or the Lone Star State, as it is affectionately and widely known – is the second largest U.S. state in both area and population^{**}, spanning no less than an astonishing 268,820 square miles, and with an ever-increasing population that is currently in excess of 24 million. Houston is its largest city and the fourth largest in the United States, while Dallas–Fort Worth is the biggest metropolitan area in the state and the fourth largest in the nation. Other major cities in this highly diverse and multi-cultural state include San Antonio, and the capital: Austin.

Texas contains both colorful and majestic landscapes, resembling in places both the Deep South and the desert south-west. Certainly, traveling from east to west, one can quite easily observe piney woods and large, semi-forests of oak and cross timbers, rolling plains and prairie, and finally the desert of the Big Bend.

But that is not all: all across Texas there lurks a wide array of monsters, mysterious beasts and diabolical creatures that science tells us do not exist – but that a significant percentage of the good folk of Texas most certainly know otherwise.

Indeed, in the packed pages of *Monsters of Texas*, you will learn a great deal about countless bizarre critters, including the following:

- Giant winged-things: feathered batmen, huge birds, pterodactyl-like beasts, and glowing-eyed gargoyle-style entities that haunt the Texas-Mexico border and seemingly just about everywhere else in the Lone Star State;
- Texas's very own version of Puerto Rico's infamous vampire-like monster, the blood-

---

** Alaska is the largest state by area, and California by population

sucking and marauding Chupacabras;
- Blood-thirsty, predatory werewolves said to be roaming the wilds of Texas by the eerie light of a full moon – and just occasionally by daylight, too;
- Texan equivalents of the famous Loch Ness Monster of Scotland: those water-based beasts of unknown origin and identity that occasionally surface from the murky depths to strike both terror and amazement into the hearts and minds of those that cross their watery paths;
- The infamous legend of the hairy wild man, and wild woman, of the Navidad that struck terror into the minds and souls of the people of the area way back in the 1800s;
- Encounters of the distinctly Bigfoot kind in central and east Texas, as well as in the state's legendary and mysterious Big Thicket woods;
- Out-of-place animals: those creatures that are found within the Lone Star State, yet that have apparently strayed – sometimes inexplicably so – far away from their normal habitats;
- A catalog of truly ominous beasts that may be far less than flesh and blood in nature, and far more paranormal and supernatural in origin;
- The diabolical, cloven-hoofed Goat Men that haunt the dark woods of Lake Worth, the old Alton Bridge at Denton, and the city of Dallas's White Rock Lake;

And, of course, much more of a truly Texan and monstrous nature!

We invite you to read on – if you dare, of course…

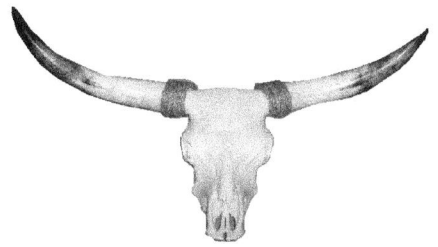

Chapter I

Big Bird and Other Winged Monsters

(Ken Gerhard)

During the spring of 2007, my book *Big Bird! Modern Sightings of Flying Monsters* was published. In the course of doing my many and varied investigations, I was very intrigued to discover that there have been numerous reports of gigantic, winged creatures throughout south Texas for decades, with the vast majority occurring during the 1970s in and around the Rio Grande Valley.

Certainly, the descriptions vary to some extent, with one group characterizing the birds as enormous black raptors that closely resemble condors, while the other group draws comparisons with the long-extinct, flying reptiles known as pterosaurs. At the time of the publication of my book, I wondered if it might very possibly open up a magical floodgate of new reports, since many people do tend to be influenced by the power of suggestion. Or, as is often the case, some find such a climate very conducive to coming forward with their own, previously repressed experiences.

Before too long, a producer named Beth Pacunas, who was working for the television show *Monster Quest* contacted me. *Monster Quest* was the History Channel's highly successful cryptozoology series that is overseen by executive producer and Bigfoot enthusiast Doug Hajicek. At the time, Beth was in the process of doing research for an episode on the legendary Thunderbirds of North America. These creatures are likened to enormous eagles and are prominent in numerous, Native American folklores and totems. The name Thunderbird is derived from the sound that is apparently produced as a result of the thunderous beating of the mighty wings of the creature. Surprisingly, these mythological beasts are occasionally still reportedly seen flying around in our modern skies, and, incredibly, are described as having wingspans comparable to that of a small airplane, no less. Needless to say, I eagerly and quickly accepted Beth's offer to appear on *Monster Quest*, where I was to discuss the many remarkable Texas-based sightings that had crossed my path over the years. In short order, she arranged to fly down in order to interview me, as well as to speak with some of the Big Bird eyewitnesses who reside in the Valley.

During the summer of 2007, Beth and her cameraman caught a flight down from Minnesota and we drove south from my home in San Antonio to the Mexican border. Our first stop was the San Benito neighborhood known as La Colonia, where truly amazing encounters with monstrous, devil birds have been documented for a number of decades. Following a video-taped interview with local researcher and Big Bird eyewitness Guadalupe Cantu III, Beth attempted to get my commentary as I stood next to a sweltering, mosquito-infested Resaca. Alas, wholly unable to deal with the absolute swarm of insects, we ultimately settled on the much more preferable comfort of an air-conditioned hotel room for my interview. While at the Resaca, however, I was quite fortunate enough to catch a glimpse of a very large Jabiru stork: a rare, migratory bird that has been suggested as an explanation for at least some of the Big Bird reports and encounters.

Following a hearty and very welcome dinner, we headed over to a nearby *Denny's* for a meeting of the *Enlightenment Society*, a local group that is organized and coordinated by author Lynn David Livsey and that discusses a wide range of anomalous events on a weekly basis. It was my firm hope that we would run into society member and Big Bird eyewitness Alex Resendez. And, as luck would have it, Resendez was indeed in attendance on that very evening, and was persuaded to talk to us about two different sightings he claimed to have had during the 1970s. We then headed back to our hotel rooms in order to get some much needed rest, but the next day I learned that late on the previous night, Beth and her cameraman had decided to film a dramatic recreation of Guadalupe Cantu's sighting – and with the waiter from the South American restaurant at which we had eaten playing the part of Guadalupe!

The episode of *Monster Quest*, which was given the colorful and memorable subtitle of *Birdzilla* (as a tribute to a certain legendary Japanese movie-monster, of course), aired in November of 2007, and I was quite pleased with the way it all turned out. In addition to addressing the Big Bird phenomenon, the show also focused upon reports of gigantic raptors from both Illinois and Alaska. The episode included the famous Lawndale incident, in which an Illinois youth named Marlon Lowe was snatched up by a large condor-like bird in front of several onlookers, including his horrified mother. It was truly fascinating to listen to Marlon, by now a grown man, describing the absolute terror that he had experienced prior to escaping from the clutches of his winged attacker on July 25, 1977.

Following my work for *Monster Quest*, a reporter named Annie McCormack, who was piecing together a story for Albuquerque's *Eyewitness News*, got in touch with me. Annie explained to me how a gentleman named David Zander claimed to have had a most disturbing encounter in New Mexico's Dona Ana Mountains at some point during the mid 1980s. While out hiking in familiar territory, Zander spotted two very pronounced figures that were perched upon the top of a good-sized bluff in the distance. As David drew near to them, the dark, man-sized figures began to take flight, and David no doubt wondered if he would possibly end up as a menu item later that day. Instead, fortunately, the two enormous birds soared off over the desert. David decided to report his sighting to the authorities, since the birds most resembled gigantic vultures and could reasonably pose a very real threat to others.

Annie initially wanted to arrange an on-camera interview with me in New Mexico. But, due to the lack of budget for what was to be only a two-minute segment, they instead decided to dispatch a crew from my local affiliate, ironically named *KENS5*. Well-known San Antonio television reporter Joe Conger, who I had watched before in a whole variety of scenarios (from wading through flooded streets, to confronting corrupt officials) called me in order to arrange a time and day for the interview. Within a week, Conger had stopped by my apartment, along with a tall cameraman, named Jerry, in order to conduct the question and answer session. As things progressed, Joe became highly intrigued, while I recounted reports of strange, flying beasts, and which I had carefully collected throughout south Texas and, even in the Alamo City. At the conclusion, Joe suggested that perhaps it would be highly advantageous for *KENS5* to produce its very own story focusing on the Texas sightings.

In July of 2007, Annie McCormack's Thunderbird story was broadcast in Albuquerque, with the San Antonio segment airing soon afterwards. Both pieces contained interviews with eye-witness David Zander, in addition to myself and noted skeptic Benjamin Radford. The Texas broadcast also included Guadalupe Cantu, who told how he and a relative had come across an eight foot tall black raptor perched on a telephone pole near Rangerville, Texas during the 1990s. Guadalupe, who had first appeared as a youthful researcher in the classic cryptozoology book, *Creatures of the Outer Edge,* by Jerome Clark and Loren Coleman, had been instrumental in helping me to gather many eyewitness sightings for my book, in addition to being a very important contact for me in the Valley too.

After the local broadcast ran I was informed by Joe Conger that the subsequent posting of the story on the internet drew well over 100,000 hits worldwide, which was truly fantastic news. Apparently, people all over the globe were fascinated by the Big Bird phenomenon – and rightly so too. And, as a result of the segment's overwhelming popularity, I participated in a follow-up story for *KENS5* during the following November. Conger had told me that a number of eyewitnesses had contacted the station following the first broadcast, and added that he would be more than happy to put me in touch with all of them. In addition, I decided to return to the Valley and mount a digital camera on the roof of the Cantu residence, in hopes of potentially capturing an invaluable image of the elusive bird that was said to frequent his neighborhood. Sadly, Guadalupe passed away quite unexpectedly in 2008, only mere months after his television appearances.

As a specific part of the November broadcast, San Antonio resident Frank Ramirez agreed to share his dramatic story with the world at large. It is one that truly teeters upon the edge of your very worst nightmares. Ramirez told Conger that he had heard loud noises emanating from the roof of his garage on the city's south side one particular evening, and when he went outside to investigate, he was horrified to discover a large dark figure perched ominously upon the roof. The figure appeared to lift up its giant wings and unfurl them in a truly menacing and terrifying fashion when confronted by Ramirez. Overcome with cold, stark fear, Frank turned and ran away as fast as he possibly could; all the while hearing loud sounds that closely resembled a large sheet flapping in the wind.

Perhaps the most bizarre aspects of this case, however, are the sketches drawn by the eyewitness, following his encounter. Ramirez, evidently a highly gifted artist, portrayed his macabre and uninvited visitor as having an elongated, humanoid face that was stretched down in the shape of a long bill, and which made it look like some vile thing that had loomed straight out of the dark pages of an H.P. Lovecraft story. In addition, the subject of his illustrations seems to be wearing some kind of enormous cloak, rather than having an actual pair of wings. Strangely enough, the entity somewhat resembled descriptions of another famous Texas mystery creature known as the Houston Batman: a 1950s monster, and about which much more in a future chapter of this book.

I was able to speak with Frank Ramirez by phone very soon after his interview had aired. He explained to me that the incident had occurred around 1998, at approximately three o'clock in the morning. Ramirez swore to me that he was not under the influence of any drugs or alcohol at the time, although he had entertained some friends earlier in the evening. A week prior to Frank's encounter, an intruder had apparently attempted to break into his home via a window, so quite understandably he had cautiously crept out to his yard in order to investigate the strange noises. When his eyes adjusted to the darkness, he caught something in his peripheral vision, sitting on the top of his garage. Ramirez told me that: "The thing was huge and black… unbelievable. There was no reflection of light upon it."

He also confirmed that he had heard a loud flapping sound while he was running away, and that the tops of the nearby pecan trees seemed to tremble as the beast passed by. Ramirez later asked his neighbors if anyone else had seen anything unusual that night, but no-one had, unfortunately. He and I agreed to set up a later date for a more in depth interview, but when I attempted to call him back a week or so later, there was nothing aside from dead air on the other end of the telephone line. Perhaps Frank Ramirez saw something that he wasn't supposed to. The mystery remains precisely that: a mystery.

Another eyewitness who contacted *KENS5* was a woman who had expressed deep relief upon learning that others had reported seeing flying monsters over San Antonio. "Because of your story, I know that I am not crazy," Blanca Trevino confessed in an emotion-filled email to the station.

When I interviewed her, she still seemed deeply affected by her amazing sighting. Blanca is an employee of the local water management team in San Antonio's Southside district. She told me that one summer's day in 2007, she had just gotten off of work and was driving near FM 1937 and Valley Road when, without warning, she was startled to the core by an enormous black bird that was taking to the skies from a wooded area to her direct left. For a brief moment, Blanca lost sight of the strange animal. But then, suddenly, it reappeared directly in front of her. Indeed, to her horror the creature seemed to be heading right towards her windshield.

Above: The legendary Thunderbird (Nick Redfern)
Below: Monterrey mountains and flying monsters (Nick Redfern)

Native American totem pole featuring stylised bird

She later admitted to me that, at first, she'd considered the possibility she might be hallucinating since she was pregnant at the time and thought that perhaps her hormones were causing her to have an overactive imagination, however highly unlikely such a scenario might seem upon sober reflection. As the thing got closer, however, Blanca became convinced that what she was seeing was all too real. She described the bird to me as being huge, extremely ugly, and very nasty looking indeed.

As it drew near to her, Blanca estimated that the animal's wings were each five to six feet across and that its head was approximately comparable in size to that of a German shepherd. She thought the bird's beak resembled that of a parrot, though somewhat more elongated, and said that its eyes looked like those typical of an owl. Overall, Blanca thought that the creature was scarier than any bird she had ever seen in her life and much more so than any vulture. At the very last second, she even let out a scream and veered off the road, in order to avoid a collision with the frightening winged-thing.

Being of Mexican-American heritage, Blanca immediately thought of Lechuza, which is a very famous legend throughout south Texas. In local folklore, Lechuza is regarded as a witch who can transform herself into the shape of a great giant bird while very often retaining some noticeably human attributes and qualities. It is considered to be a very bad omen for those who have the misfortune to see the crone-like Lechuza and to cross her path.

After her encounter, Blanca was so freaked out that she felt "crazy", but she still told her husband about her unnerving experience. When she saw the broadcast on *KENS5*, Blanca was immensely relieved to hear that others in Texas had reported similar encounters, and felt compelled to write to the station about her sighting. Even to this day, she admits to still being afraid to drive by the spot where the strange incident occurred. Such is the terrifying and long-standing effect that beasts of this type can have on a person's mind, heart and soul.

One thing that Blanca was not aware of is the fact that the location of her encounter is only two miles from where one of the most famous of all Big Bird sightings took place. During the morning of February 24, 1976, three teachers from the Southside School District claimed that they observed two enormous prehistoric-looking birds, which resembled the ancient flying reptiles called pterodactyls. The utterly amazed trio even pulled their separate cars over to the side of the road in order to try and get a better look at the plane-sized creatures that soared majestically and proudly overhead. The teachers were so perplexed and baffled by their sighting that they immediately decided to contact the local newspapers, and indeed their sighting made headlines the following day. Perhaps not wanting to alarm the students, however, the school district's board-members quickly silenced the teachers, sternly warning them never to discuss the incident again.

A report which I found on the internet after my *Big Bird!* book had already gone to press was posted on a popular cryptozoology website by a woman named Debbie Fisher. Debbie had written that she had been living in an apartment complex on the north-west side of San Antonio during the mid 1980s, when she and her brother sighted something highly unusual indeed – and that's putting it extremely mildly, to say the very least!

On a warm summer's eve, the pair had been outside looking at the stars and talking when they noticed a large, winged creature gliding above the utility lines that hung overhead. Both of them thought that there was something extremely abnormal about the animal, since its large, silhouetted wings appeared both angular and reptilian in nature and appearance. It most certainly didn't resemble any kind of bird that they had ever seen before. The thing was gliding back and forth and seemed to be watching them in what they perceived to be a very menacing fashion; something that caused the pair to feel both understandably uncomfortable and highly disturbed. This went on for about ten minutes or so, until Debbie and her brother sensibly agreed that it might be a very good idea for them to go back inside the apartment.

Fortunately, I was able to track down Debbie Fisher and I phoned her one evening in order to try and gather more information about what it was that she and her brother had seen on that fateful night all those years ago. Debbie told me that when the incident occurred in the mid-1980s, she was in her early twenties and her brother had been a teenager. At the time, their family had been living in an apartment complex that still to this day stands near the intersection of Huebner and Babcock roads in San Antonio (which, coincidentally and ironically, lies very close to where I live at the time of this writing). The area is fairly developed now, although Debbie described it as being quite a different place at the time and largely rural in both nature and appearance. She and her brother always enjoyed going outside in the warm, summer evenings, Debbie told me. They would look at the stars and talk about life.

Debbie recalled that both of them had noticed the strange animal at the same, precise time. It was flying back and forth just above the utility lines across the street and seemed to have a wingspan that approached ten feet. As the interview continued, Debbie explained to me how she had previously lived in Florida, where she had an ample opportunity to observe a wide variety of large birds.

This particular creature, however, most definitely did not resemble anything that she had ever seen before. The silhouetted outline of its wings appeared to be "more bat-like than bird-like" to her, and it actually made her feel both "creepy and uncomfortable", as if she was in some kind of vampire movie. Overall, Debbie felt that the thing resembled a pterodactyl more than anything else she could think of. After about ten minutes, the two siblings mutually agreed that there was something strange about the creature that was darkly and deeply menacing. They understandably became "freaked out", and so quickly went inside to avoid any potential threat. The incident was over.

An extremely similar San Antonio-based report came from a college student who didn't want to receive any publicity, so I will give her the pseudonym of Mary. Like Debbie, what Mary described to me was not really reminiscent of a bird so much, but in fact most resembled the previously referred to, and presumed-extinct, flying reptiles known as pterosaurs.

Mary wrote me that back in 2004, she was returning home from college near Shavano Park along Loop 1604, when she spotted "a huge flying thing that looked more like a bat than a bird" passing overhead. Mary, who interestingly enough has a degree in biology, stated: "I really believe that this was not a bird. It looked more bat like, especially the wings and tail.

So, I know for a fact that what I saw was not a bird… prehistoric."

Mary explained how she had told her entire family about her sighting, but that at first they didn't believe her, which is, sadly, the response many witnesses to unknown creatures unfortunately receive when they decide to confide in others.

I was also contacted by a San Antonio resident named Benjamin Aum, who wrote me to say that he had seen the infamous Big Bird as a young man during the 1970s. In addition, Benjamin was sure that he and his wife had seen the shadow of an enormous bird passing over their car twice within the past year, no less. Of course, very eager to elicit yet further details on the matter, I duly met with the Ben and his wife Cris, who work as holistic healers at their metaphysical boutique on San Antonio's south-side. Upon arrival, I was greeted by audio recordings of a droning chant, as well as the smell of ritualistic incense, which had the combined effect of putting me into a tranquil, relaxed state of mind and attitude.

Benjamin and I sat in his office and discussed the possibility that he and Cris might be more in tune with the world of the supernatural due to their line of work. Indeed, they told me about two, unrelated paranormal experiences in which they had been involved. One centered upon a mystifying quilt they owned. Incredibly, its trim had been braiding itself, presumably at the hand of unknown and unseen forces, over the course of several years. The other experience involved a stolen religious article that had been returned to them under mystifying circumstances.

Aum explained to me that he had first seen the Big Bird as a youth, while at the historical Mission Espada aqueduct, where the San Antonio River has been diverted for agricultural use since the time of Spanish rule. For several minutes, he had observed an enormous black bird flying over the tops of a group of pecan trees that were situated about 100 yards away. Although Benjamin could not make out its features very well, he was quite sure that the animal's wingspan approached 15 to 20 feet across, with its overall mass seemingly comparable in size to that of a full-size pick-up truck! In other words, it was a true monster. Notably, he could tell the thing was covered in feathers, not at all like the pterosaur-style beasts that so many other witnesses have memorably described to me over the years.

Much more recently, Benjamin and Cris were driving on San Antonio's south-side, when they suddenly became aware of a huge bird-shaped shadow that engulfed their car. The couple was in complete and utter disbelief, because the shadow seemed to actually span the width of the entire road. In fact, they immediately pulled over and jumped out of their vehicle, fully expecting to catch a glimpse of a gigantic bird. Instead, they were astonished to find that the creature was nowhere in sight at all. At the conclusion of our intriguing meeting, Benjamin theorized that perhaps these birds could be traveling in and out of some kind of vortex or another dimension even, a view that has certainly been expressed by others whose lives have been touched, affected and forever changed by the Big Bird.

Wherever they're actually from, these winged enigmas are making their presence known elsewhere in Texas too. As hard evidence of this, I received a letter from a woman living in Round

Rock who wishes to remain anonymous. I'll call her Karen. She wrote me to say that she and her daughter were driving home at around two in the morning, during April or May of 2000, when they encountered "one of these birds close up". Karen had just picked up her daughter from work and they were traveling north on Parmer Highway, just north of Austin, when a massive bird suddenly swooped right over the roof of their car.

Karen stated: "It was so close that I could make out small, roundish-looking gray-colored feathers on its body. I couldn't see its head. This bird was huge – as big as my car. Its wing-span must have been at least 10 to 15 feet. I was shocked and couldn't believe what I was seeing. I thought maybe I was still sleepy, so I turned to my daughter to see if she had seen it too and she said that she had."

Karen's daughter then confessed to me that she had seen a similar, but even larger, bird around a year earlier, while driving with a friend on Austin's Highway 183. If these big birds are, in fact, some type of paranormal phenomenon, rather than being purely flesh and blood in nature, perhaps it would go some significant way towards explaining why a number of people have claimed multiple sightings, rather than just one.

Karen's letter concluded: "This was like no bird that I have ever seen before. It looked big enough to carry someone off, so I didn't try to stop and get a better look. And it was just gliding along, not flapping its wings. I tried to tell a couple of people at work about it, but they thought I was crazy or seeing things. But I know what I saw. It was close enough that could see the detail of its feathers. If I had been standing on the car roof, I could have reached up and touched it."

Karen had apparently been very relieved to hear about the sightings in San Antonio, because finally she knew she was no longer alone.

Another report that I received was from a woman who I'll call Christie Duncan, and who presently resides in Upshur County in the far north-eastern corner of the state. Christie had seen me on television speaking about the Big Bird sightings and had decided to write to me following her sighting which happened on January 12, 2008. Mrs. Duncan felt compelled to contact me after she spotted an enormous black bird flying over her pasture one particular afternoon.

Christie told me the following: "I see crows and turkey vultures on a daily basis here in the piney woods, even a bald eagle pair. But, this I saw was much larger than anything I have ever seen. I ran and told my teenage daughter what I saw. She didn't believe me, so I called my husband at work and told him. Again, he didn't believe me either. He thought I was telling a big bass tale, you know, the one that got away."

She went on to explain: "At the south end of our property, there is 170 acres with a pine tree grove that is about 15 years old. This is what I used to get a perspective on the bird's size. The bird's wingspan outreached several of these pine tops. I was about 300 yards away and it still looked massive." Like the majority of the eyewitnesses who have contacted me, Christie expressed a keen desire to confide in someone who would believe her story and treat it in a serious fashion, which of course is precisely what I did.

Returning to the Rio Grande Valley, where the vast majority of all the Big Bird sightings have occurred and where they are continuing to occur, there is an account from an Eagle Scout named Joseph Hasse, who lives in Brownsville. Joseph described to me how he and a friend had seen something very weird one evening while sitting in their car in the Rio Del Sol subdivision along FM 511. Hasse happened to glance up and noticed a reflection of something unknown flying in the night sky, at which point he quickly alerted his friend to its monstrous and gigantic presence.

At first, the two teens thought that the form just might possibly be an airplane, but they didn't see any lights. When they got out of the car in an attempt to get a better look, the youths realized that the object was actually much closer than they initially thought, but was making no noise at all. Joseph and his friend realized that it was a living creature when, without any sort of warning at all, it flew in a semi-circle and began to flap its huge wings, changing direction as it vanished over the horizon. After gaining their composure and comparing notes, both teens were in complete agreement that what they saw resembled, in their very own words: "A bat-like creature with ribbed wings, no feathers, a long pointed beak, a long pointed devil-shaped tail and a wingspan of roughly about 12 feet."

An admittedly-vague, and anonymous, report from the internet, described how another individual had seemingly spotted a Thunderbird in the Valley. The witness characterized the bird as being chocolate-colored and about five or six feet tall, with a 12 to 15 foot wingspan. Another Valley resident (from McAllen) told of how, when she was 10 years old back in the early 1990s, she, along with several of the neighborhood children, saw a gigantic bird flying over, something which actually causing the trees underneath to noticeably sway. The huge creature apparently landed on a nearby billboard, where all of those who were present observed it for a couple of minutes, apparently in total awe. The mother of one of the children came outside to see what all the commotion was about and declared that the animal had to have been a Thunderbird. Eventually, an approaching 18-wheeler caused the bird to fly away and out of sight. Supposedly, the truck even came to a screeching stop and its driver jumped out and shouted: "That is some crazy [*expletive*]!"

Adam Moran of San Antonio wrote to me after he read an article about the San Antonio Big Bird sightings. He declared that: "At the intersection of Seneca and Evers, I saw an absolutely enormous bird land in the middle of the road. I was about 50 to 100 yards away, but it resembled a turkey vulture, but much bigger. Judging from the van that stopped when it landed (nobody hits their brakes for a pigeon), it was at least three feet tall." Adam summarized by stating: "When it took off again, the wings were so enormous that I could see them ripple… if the wings were less than 10 to 12 feet I'd be shocked." Adam's overall impression was that the bird resembled a California condor. This sighting apparently took place relatively recently: on May 12, 2008.

There is also the case of a young man named Josh. While bike riding with his father in the Valley High area of San Antonio, Josh told me that he and his father stopped near a big, blue water tower near their house, when they looked up at the structure and noticed "a huge thing with glowing red eyes, huge wings and thorns sticking out of the wings… and horns on his head." He and his father were not able to make out much else in the way of details, because: "The figure was pitch black."

But, they were absolutely astounded by the monster's great size, since it appeared to be half as big as the water tower upon which it was perched! Just as Josh reached for his phone to take a picture, the apparition flew away and out of sight.

The most recent report of which I am aware, as of this writing at least, is from an associate named Jym Evans, who has been interested in cryptozoology for years. Jym left a dramatic message on my answer machine during October of 2008, explaining how he had been kayaking down the San Marcos River with a friend, when they startled a very unusual animal, causing it to fly away over a group of trees. They were both taken aback when they noted the size of the bird-like creature. Jym estimated that the thing had at least an eight foot wingspan. Both were sure that whatever the mighty animal was, it was completely devoid of feathers, but possessed leathery skin, rather like that of a reptile, and a pair of very angular wings. Significantly, they both thought that it very closely resembled a classic pterosaur.

Regardless of whether these winged monsters are indeed survivors from prehistoric times, renegade condors, or phantom flyers from another dimension that co-exists with – and sometimes crosses paths with – our own, of only one thing can we be truly certain: Texans, all around the state, are continuing to have encounters with flying unknowns that the world of science has totally overlooked, ignored and rejected for far too long.

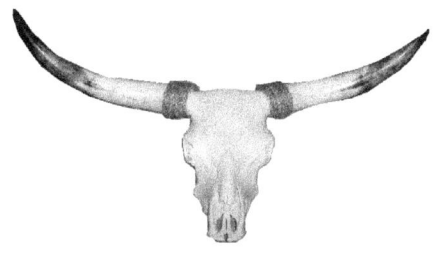

Chapter II
Lone Star Werewolves

(Nick Redfern)

E ven a man who is pure of heart and says his prayers by night, may become a wolf when the wolf bane blooms and the autumn moon is bright," was the eerie message immortalized in the classic 1941 film, *The Wolf-man*. And it's a message that many have taken, and continue to take, extremely seriously. For those who firmly believe in the existence of literal werewolves, the stark image of the hairy shape-shifting beast that is part-human and part-wolf, and that proceeds to embark upon a marauding killing spree at the sight of a full moon, is most certainly no joke.

But if such creatures really do exist in our world, are they true werewolves of the type that have been so successfully brought to the big-screen time and again by Hollywood movie moguls and special effects experts? Could they possibly be deranged souls, afflicted by a variety of both mental illnesses and deep delusions? Or might they even have distinctly paranormal origins? Paradoxically, the answer to all three of those controversial questions might very well be a definitive: "Yes."

Clinical lycanthropy is a very rare psychiatric condition which is typified by an overwhelming delusion that the afflicted person has the ability to morph into the form of a wild animal – and very often that of a berserk, killer-wolf, and usually one of monstrous proportions too. Interestingly, a 1999 paper titled *Lycanthropy: New Evidence of its Origin* written by H.F. Moselhy, demonstrated that two people diagnosed with clinical lycanthropy displayed evidence of unusual activity in the parts of the brain known to be involved in representing how we perceive body shape and image. In other words, clinical lycanthropes might very well really believe that their bodies are mutating when they are overwhelmed by their delusions – even if such changes are not noticeable to anyone else.

Of course, this does not fully explain why so many such people believe they are changing into one specific animal – such as a wolf – rather than just experiencing random changes in, say, their arms or legs. But nevertheless, it is without doubt a significant part of the overall werewolf controversy. And there is another aspect to this affair that may go some way towards explaining the inner workings of the mind of the clinical lycanthrope.

Linda Godfrey, a leading and recognized authority on werewolves in the United States, and who lives in pleasant and rural Wisconsin, says: "One other medical explanation that turns up frequently in relation to lycanthropy is the ergot equation. A fungus that affects rye, ergot is now widely regarded as a possible cause of the bestial madness. According to this theory, it was not demonic influence but the ingestion of *Claviceps purpurea* (which contains a compound similar to LSD), which led to the demented behavior. All it took was a cold winter in a particularly wet or low-lying area, and entire fields would be infected with the ergot fungus."

She continues: "Symptoms, confirmed by an outbreak as recent as the 1950s in France, include delusions of turning into hairy monsters, night terrors, a sense of alienation from one's own body, frantic motion and convulsions, paranoia, and even death."

Beyond any shadow of doubt at all, one of the most notorious serial killers of all time was Peter Stumpp, a German farmer who became infamously known as the *Werewolf of Bedburg*. Born in the village of Epprath, Cologne, Stumpp was a wealthy, respected, and influential farmer in the local community. But he was also hiding a truly dark and diabolical secret – one that surfaced graphically and sensationally in 1589, when he was brought to trial for the heinous crimes of both murder and cannibalism.

Having been subjected to the extreme torture of the rack, Stumpp confessed to countless horrific acts, including feasting on the flesh of sheep, lambs and goats, and even that of men, women and children too. Indeed, Stumpp further revealed that he had killed and devoured no less than 14 children, two pregnant women and their fetuses, and even his own son's brain. Stumpp, however, had an extraordinary excuse to try and explain and account for his vile actions.

Stumpp maintained that since the age of 12, he had secretly engaged in black magic, and on one occasion had succeeded in summoning up none other than the Devil, who provided him with a "magical belt" that gave him the ability to shape-shift into "the likeness of a greedy, devouring wolf, strong and mighty, with eyes great and large, which in the night sparkled like fire, a mouth great and wide, with most sharp and cruel teeth, a huge body, and mighty paws."

While the Devil may well have been impressed and satisfied by Stumpp's explanation, the court most assuredly was not, and he was put to death in brutal fashion: flesh was torn from his body, his arms and legs were broken, and, finally, he was beheaded. The *Werewolf of Bedburg* was no more. Stumpp was not alone however.

Equally as horrific as the actions of Peter Stumpp were those of an un-named man who, in the final years of the 16th Century, became known as the *Werewolf of Chalons*. A Paris, France-based tailor who killed, dismembered, and ate the flesh of numerous children he had lured into his shop, he was brought to trial for his crimes on December 14, 1598. Notably, during the trial, it was claimed that on occasion the man also roamed nearby woods in the form of a huge, predatory wolf, where he further sought out innocent souls to both slaughter and consume. As was the case with Stumpp, the Werewolf of Chalons was sentenced to death and duly burned at the stake.

The idea that mental illness – possibly accompanied by the ingestion of ergot – could account for some of the legends of werewolf activity is highly plausible and very likely. But not every-one is quite so certain that this scenario can lay the entire matter of lycanthropy to rest. Before digging deeply into the controversial matter of the modern-day Texas Werewolves, I decided to do some preliminary background research in both local libraries and newspaper archives and discovered, to my great surprise, that Texas had a rich history and folklore of all things diabolical, hairy and wolfish. For example, in 1845, at the Devil's River near Del Rio, south-west Texas, a young boy living at San Felipe Springs described viewing a group of over-sized wolves that – along with a long-haired, and distinctly unkempt, young girl – were violently attacking a herd of terrified goats.

Not surprisingly, concerned townsfolk rapidly initiated a search for both the girl and the beasts. After 72 hours, she was seen yet again and was finally cornered in a canyon. As was the case on the previous occasion, the girl was not alone. That's right: the same pack of vi-cious wolves was with her – one of which was quickly shot and killed after it suddenly lunged at a member of the posse. As the remaining wolves quickly retreated, the men moved in and succeeded in capturing the girl, who was then taken to the confines of a locked room at a nearby ranch. Of course, there was far more to come.

After darkness had well and truly set in, the wolf pack set their sights on the ranch. Displaying a seemingly high degree of intelligence and uncanny cunning, they slowly closed in on the building and ominously surrounded it on all sides. Not surprisingly, the farm animals became highly agitated; confusion and fear reigned supreme as the wolves attacked, and the girl suc-ceeded in making good her escape amidst all the mayhem and chaos. For an astonishing seven years, she successfully remained elusive and overwhelmingly avoided capture.

But the girl was seen once more: in 1852, a team of surveyors that was looking to construct a new route to El Paso saw her crouched on a sandbar on the Rio Grande; this time she was with two wolf pups. Keenly aware that they were being watched, the trio quickly vanished into the surrounding woods, never to be seen again.

Was the girl merely a feral child; one who had gone wild and was raised in the wilderness by a pack of wolves that had allowed her to enter their elite world? Might she have been a defini-tive shape-shifting lycanthrope? Or was she something else entirely? More than 150 years later, those questions remain unanswered. And, they are very likely to remain that way too – unless, perhaps, one day the skeletal remnants of a human female are unearthed near the Rio

Grande, closely surrounded by the bones of her equally long-deceased animalistic family and friends...

The June 2, 1888 edition of the *Dallas Morning News* told a strange tale with the eye-catching headline of *A Huge Wolf Killed, Big as a Yearling*. According to the journalist that wrote the story: "Frank Boshore, a farmer living near the city, killed and brought to town yesterday one of the largest gray wolves that was [sic] ever killed in this country. It was nearly as tall as a yearling calf. These animals have been a great disadvantage to the community, one man saying that he had been damaged at least $1,000 by them on sheep."

Is it perhaps feasible that a number of early encounters with werewolves in Texas were, actually, misidentifications of very real wolves, albeit ones of a truly monstrous nature and scale, such as that described by the Dallas Morning News in June 1888? Perhaps we should give this theory some particular and deep consideration.

For example, in the packed pages of her acclaimed title *Hunting the American Werewolf*, author and researcher Linda Godfrey offered the theory that a number of unidentified animals seen in the wilds of the United States and presumed to be werewolves might, in reality, have been still-surviving packs of animals known collectively as *Amphicyonidae*, which translates as: "dogs of doubtful origin". A truly terrifying and ferocious combination of large bear and muscular dog, one such beast that squarely fell into this group was the Amphicyon, a very strong, imposing and lethal predator that lived during the Miocene era, some twenty three to five million years ago, after which time it became extinct. Or, maybe it didn't...

Hunt for Phantom-Like Animal was the bold heading that leapt off the front page of the January 29, 1908 issue of the *Dallas Morning News*. The newspaper recorded that an unknown, large creature – that some described as resembling a massive dog and others said was nothing less than a huge wolf – was causing overwhelming carnage across the city of Waco, and had been up to its infernal activities for at least four weeks.

Farm animals were being eaten by the dozen, and dark rumors began to surface suggesting that the creature might actually have paranormal or other-worldly origins, rather than ones of a definitively flesh and blood nature. A staff writer for the *Dallas Morning News* recorded that one person whose path had unfortunately crossed with the animal said it seemed to pass "like a phantom, jumping fences from one lot to another, elusive and shadowy, except where the use is made of teeth and claws."

The press additionally stated: "The McLennan County Fox Hunters' Association with their best hunters declare that while they have been able to capture big wolves, red and gray foxes, bobcats and catamounts, they are baffled by this peculiar beast."

Despite an intense search, the creature was never caught or firmly identified. And, soon after, it evidently moved on to pastures new, as the slayings came to an abrupt and mysterious halt.

Solomon's strange and nightmarish experience with what was surely a definitive werewolf

Above: The Lone Star State Werewolves (Nick Redfern)
Below: Paladora State Park, ghostly black-dog territory (Nick Redfern)

occurred in dense woodland near the Texan town of Orange way back in the 1930s – to be specific, in 1933. At the time, Solomon was a young boy, and was fishing with a couple of friends in a small brook. Without warning, the intrepid pals all developed an uncanny feeling of being watched. And their senses were not wrong. On the other side of the small stretch of water, just poking through the trees, they could see the huge and monstrous head of a giant wolf-like beast. That was, in itself, terrifying enough; however, when the beast hauled its entire form through the foliage, their terror reached stratospheric levels. Although undoubtedly some type of wolf, it was around 10 feet long, and both its jaws and legs were large and muscular in the extreme. In other words, this was no normal wolf. By definition, it was a true monster. And then, the story took on very strange, perhaps even supernatural, overtones.

When I interviewed Solomon a few years ago, the now aged man told me that after he and his friends had spent a couple of minutes utterly rooted to the spot with a mixture of overwhelming fear and a high degree of awe and curiosity as it paced back and forth in what was perceived to be a restless manner, the mighty beast promptly sat down on the grass, and its body began to quickly vibrate in a truly strange fashion that Solomon described as "wrong and horrible." At the same time, the beast became shrouded in a light green-colored mist that seemed to rise up from the ground directly below the animal, shortly after which the vibrating stopped, and the great creature rose up onto its hind legs and slowly headed back into the trees.

Of course, there are not – or there most certainly should not be – any bipedal wolves anywhere in the world, never mind in the woods of Texas! Yet, decades later, Solomon is absolutely adamant that for a few brief minutes he and his friends were exposed to an animal that had all the characteristics of a wolf, yet that was seemingly able to prowl around the countryside "both like a man and the animals". No-one should be surprised to learn that Solomon elected to stay away from those oppressive woods for the next few years.

Certainly, one of the most memorable accounts of the werewolf variety came from a Mrs. Delburt Gregg, who lived in the East Texan town of Greggton, which is situated close to Longview. Quite appropriately, it was late at night at the height of a fierce thunderstorm in the summer of 1958 when Mrs. Gregg was awoken by the noise of what sounded like scratching on her bedroom window.

Slightly flummoxed and puzzled, as a result of her still sleepy state, Mrs. Gregg wondered what was going on – that is until a flash of lightning illuminated the entire bedroom, and to her everlasting horror revealed the form of a "huge, shaggy, wolf-like creature" that stared malevolently in her direction with what was memorably described as a pair of "baleful, glowing, slitted [*sic*] eyes." The terrified Mrs. Gregg leapt out of her bed and raced to get a flashlight, but the creature had already charged off into the darkness and was lost from sight, never to return and torment the unfortunate witness again.

The tale of the lycanthrope of the town of Converse is one that is interesting, but admittedly it has classic folkloric overtones to it also. So the somewhat *friend of a friend* tale goes, at some point during the 1960s, a creature that firmly fitted the classic Hollywood image of a werewolf savagely killed a young boy in the area, and specifically at a location known by the town's inhabitants – both then and now – as Skull's Crossing. The father of the boy had sent his son on his very first – and, as it turned out, his absolute last – hunting excursion. The hunter, however, soon became the prey. As the boy tentatively made his way into an area comprised of thick tall trees, the beast loomed into view, and the petrified youngster raced for the safety of his home.

That should have been the end of the matter; unfortunately, the boy's father – determined to turn his young son into a man by introducing him to the world of hunting – simply poked fun at the boy and ordered him to return to the woods, coldly adding that he should not even think about coming home until he had killed something. Never again would father and son see each other however. After the boy had been gone for a considerable number of hours, the by-now-concerned father called the police, and a search team finally found him deep in the woods: a huge, predatory wolf-like beast was straddling his body, savagely tearing off chunks of flesh and crunching down on the boy's bones.

Even to this day, the tale of the Converse werewolf is very well known throughout the town itself; however, no-one today is apparently able to identify the tragic family concerned – something which suggests that while we should not outright dismiss the tale, we should at least be aware of the possibility that it may very well just be the Converse equivalent of the many similar tales and legends that dominate little villages, hamlets and towns all across the globe, and that have done so for centuries.

Paradise is a small town, situated not too far from the sprawling city of Fort Worth, but one that is dominated by isolated homes, thick and somewhat mysterious woods, sprawling fields, numerous cows, and not much more at all. Aside from perhaps a killer werewolf, that is.

Dawn had just broken on a particular day in September 1996, and Walter, a rancher who had made Paradise his home, headed out to tend his cows, which had the run of a large field at the back of his property. Walter was certainly not expecting to find the horrifying scene upon which he stumbled: one of his most valuable cows had been killed under cover of darkness. And by the looks of the cow, the killer had been some sort of vicious powerful creature that surely had no place prowling the fields of Paradise. The cow was disemboweled with its throat ripped out and both back legs completely gone.

Although Walter wasted no time in contacting the police, this turned out to be an utterly fruitless task, since the only thing that the responding officers could suggest to the irate and worried rancher was that perhaps a big cat was responsible for the atrocity and was still on the loose. And while this was certainly a major cause for alarm and a matter they would most definitely look into, it was not, technically speaking, a crime that required the attention of the police.

So, a wholly dissatisfied Walter decided to take matters into his own hands and elected to embark upon a night-time vigil, in the hope that the beast might return and he would have the opportunity to blow the creature's head clean off its shoulders and put an end to the matter before it risked spiraling wildly out of control.

Thus it was that at roughly 2.00 a.m. four days later, and while dutifully scanning the field with a night-scope that was attached to his high-powered gun, Walter became frozen with fear when he caught sight of a large hairy figure striding across the field. Around seven feet in height, very muscular and dark, it had the body of a man, yet the face, the ears and the muzzle of what looked like a large German shepherd dog or a wild wolf. Rooted to the spot, Walter didn't even think to fire his gun. Rather, he simply watched, dumbstruck with fear and awe as the beast covered the width of the field very quickly and vanished into the trees that border his large property.

Rather ominously, only a short time later, and in the same exact spot where he first noticed the diabolical wolf-man, Walter found in the grass a small stone carved head of a large-fanged monster with slits for eyes and flared nostrils. To this day, Walter is convinced that occultists were secretly at work in the heart of his field, possibly engaged in some unholy ancient rite or ritual, and had quite literally conjured up the beast from another realm of existence. Now, he believes, the beast is wildly on the loose in our world, free of its previous moorings and trappings, and prowling the woods and fields of Texas in search of yet more tasty morsels of the bovine kind.

Midway through 2007, a creature that has been relegated by many cryptozoological commentators to a definitively bygone era, the Ghostly hell-hound – which does have a few admitted parallels with tales and sightings of werewolves – surfaced from its darkened lair to terrify the good people of the Lone Star State.

Bob Trubshaw is one of the most learned researchers on the controversial subject of spectral black dog and hell-hound tales, and says: "The folklore of phantom black dogs is known throughout the British Isles. From the Black Shuck of East Anglia to the Mauthe Dhoog of the Isle of Man there are tales of huge spectral hounds 'darker than the night sky' with eyes 'glowing red as burning coals'. The phantom black dog of British and Irish folklore, which often forewarns of death, is part of a worldwide belief that dogs are sensitive to spirits and the approach of death, and keep watch over the dead and dying. North European and Scandinavian myths dating back to the Iron Age depict dogs as corpse eaters and the guardians of the roads to hell. Medieval folklore includes a variety of 'devil dogs' and spectral hounds."

In May 2007, I was the recipient of a phone call from a lady named Ronda, then living in the Texas Panhandle, and specifically in the city of Amarillo. As Ronda carefully told me, barely 48 hours previously, and with her daughter and son in law in tow, she ventured into the heart of a truly massive canyon, which is situated only a very brief drive from Amarillo and known as the Paladora State Park.

It was while relaxing in the park and having a nice picnic that normality was surreally interrupted. Approximately two or three hundred yards from where the trio sat, a large black dog could be seen staring in their direction, and in what all three perceived as a distinctly threatening fashion. Without warning, the dog suddenly charged. As the dog bounded ever closer its sheer size could now be seen and appreciated. The beast was, said Ronda, much bigger than any dog she had ever seen before. Indeed, she likened its scale to that of a small horse – which is truly remarkable in the extreme if her estimate was accurate. Equally terrifying was the revelation to me that the beast possessed a pair of large eyes that seemed to glow with an eerie silver-colored shimmer.

The three decided that the most appropriate action would be to flee the area as soon as possible – which they most certainly did. The dog, at that point, slowed its charge down to a mere walking pace, yet carefully shadowed them for every step of the journey back to the family car. Bizarrely, as it approached a modern-day recreation of a Native American Indian tepee that sits near the entrance to the park, the demon-hound vanished into thin air, never to return and plague Ronda again.

The Texas werewolves, however, will not remain gone for long. If their past history is anything to go by, sooner or later, those vile snarling howling/hairy monstrosities are sure to make their dark presence known once more.

Chapter III:

El Chupacabras Comes to Texas

(Ken Gerhard)

I first learned of the Texas Chupacabras from my good friend, Jon Downes. Jon is best known as a truly accomplished and colorful author who heads up Britain's Centre for Fortean Zoology: an international, full-time organization that sponsors expeditions all around the world in search of strange creatures and unknown animals. And, he's also the editor and publisher of this very book, *Monsters of Texas,* too.

I'd caught wind of the fact that Jon was going to be in San Antonio filming a pilot for a television show called *The Tracker*, in which his keen, *Sherlock Holmes*-like sleuthing skills and abilities would be firmly showcased, as he investigated various unexplained mysteries all around the globe. Despite living in Houston at the time, I'd decided that it was well worth the three hour drive in order to meet with a man who was an undoubted kindred spirit.

As we sat and drank cold *Shiner Bock* beer in the courtyard of San Antonio's haunted *Menger Hotel* one evening, Jon told me about how he had been driven to a town called Elmendorf earlier that day, in order to meet a rancher named Devin McAnally. Apparently, Mr. McAnally had dispatched an inexplicable, bluish-gray animal that had been slaughtering his chickens. After looking at some photos of its strange corpse, Jon had deduced that the creature was obviously some type of canine; beyond that he was unable to make a definitive identification. The killings had occurred back in the spring of 2004, and I later learned that noted author and confessed alien abductee Whitley Streiber had taken quite an interest in the "Elmendorf Beast" at the time, to the extent that Strieber, a San Antonio native, had mounted his own investigation in order to obtain the bones of the animal for DNA testing.

By the time I met Devin McAnally nearly four years had passed. During the early months of 2008, I was hired by producers of the History Channel's television series *Monster Quest* to investigate the so-called Chupacabras reports that were coming out of Texas. In addition to McAnally's beast, at least three other grotesque hairless dog-like animals of a very similar nature had turned up dead at various places throughout the Lone Star State during a four-year span. Although the Chupacabras sightings had actually originated in Puerto Rico back in 1995, there were some similarities present in the Texas cases.

The most unusual aspect of the reports was certainly the manner in which small livestock were being slaughtered. In Puerto Rico it had started with the deaths of goats and sheep, which were usually found with their bodies intact, but massively, or even totally on occasion, devoid of their blood. And, often, there were two tell-tale puncture wounds visible on the bodies of the victims. Local media outlets quickly adopted the name Chupacabras, which in Spanish means "goat sucker", in order to identify the vampire-like predator. It was around that time that reports of an unearthly creature began to surface, described as having gray fur or skin and standing about five feet tall, with large, red, almond-shaped eyes, a reptilian tongue, and a row of vicious-looking spikes – not unlike a punk-rock Mohawk – running down the length of its head and back. Its general form was similar to that of a kangaroo. Chickens soon became another favorite target of the Chupacabras attacks, though the hysteria in Puerto Rico faded out within a decade. As was the case with the other slain animals, the chickens were typically bled dry but not eaten, as one would expect from a typical predator like a cat or a feral dog.

Meanwhile, back in Texas, this was precisely what Devin McAnally (who lost no less than 50 chickens in the same manner over a period of a few weeks) had experienced. Devin, who has raised chickens for years, was overwhelmingly perplexed by what type of animal could be murdering his chickens and drinking their blood on such a vast scale, since it most assuredly did not fit the profile of a coyote, or indeed any other varmint, he had ever dealt with previously.

When I visited Elmendorf, a small community on the outskirts of San Antonio, I was extremely impressed with McAnally and his testimony. My first thought was that Devin reminded me of the stereotypical Texan from a John Wayne movie: lean and muscular with a distinct drawl and skin that's been hardened by years of working in the hot Lone Star State sun. Devin is descended from a long line of McAnallys in Texas, having been born and raised in the Panhandle, along with four siblings and taught to be self-sufficient by his father, a Methodist minister. What I didn't realize was that Devin has a Master's degree and has studied abroad, working as a bilingual English teacher for over 40 years in the Texas school systems. Consequently, the man possesses a keen intellect and a truly vast knowledge of Tex-Mex history and culture. He had simply decided over the course of his life that he was happiest working outdoors and raising his chickens, which he has done on his property near Elmendorf for nearly two decades.

It was during the spring of 2004 that Devin had first noticed that something very unusual was afoot. One morning, he discovered to his horror that five of his chickens had been killed during the night. But rather than having been missing or partially eaten, the remains were seemingly untouched, though eerily bloodless. Within a short time, Devin found another dozen chickens that had been killed in the same manner – all in just one evening. At first he suspected his own dog of perpetrating some kind of thrill-kill, but he had never seen a domestic dog behave in such a strange manner. On the third occasion, Devin lost more than 30 chickens in one night and decided something very strange was happening. He was most certainly not wrong.

Indeed, McAnally's suspicions were confirmed when his dog alerted him to the presence of a weird animal on his property one day. Devin barely caught a glimpse of the fleeting creature, but thought that it might very well be a feral greyhound, since three racing dogs had been discarded near his property one time. He also figured that it must be the same animal that was killing his chickens, but wasn't exactly sure what it was that he was dealing with since it moved with a very irregular gait and appeared almost blue in color. And the animal definitely didn't seem to behave like a coyote might, since it didn't seem all that intimidated by either him or his dogs.

Devin spotted the animal on two more occasions, but every time he ran inside to grab his gun, the thing would be frustratingly gone by the time he returned. Consequently, he decided to prop his .22 rifle in a tree fork and leave it there until the next time the varmint came wandering around in search of a tasty chicken or several. His gambit finally, and spectacularly, paid off one day when he was carrying some buckets of water and suddenly spotted the creature; it was eating some mulberries that had fallen from one of his trees. Devin was able to carefully and quietly sneak up and aim his rifle, dropping the animal to the ground with just one shot.

As he walked up on the dead critter with gun in hand, McAnally was completely baffled by what he saw. The creature looked to be only about 20 pounds or so in weight, and was completely bald except for a wispy black mane that ran down the length of its back. Its skin appeared to be an odd bluish color and leathery in nature, and not unlike that of an elephant, Devin thought. In addition, noticeably long fangs were protruding from the animal's mouth and it sported a long, rat-like tail and sharp claws that looked like they could inflict some very serious damage. The beast's limbs and feet seemed oddly disproportionate and there was no wound or blood visible from the bullet that it had taken. Not surprisingly, Devin approached the thing very cautiously and tentatively indeed, and fired two or three more shots into its body just in case it was only stunned. He admitted to being afraid to even touch the animal, because it was so creepy looking, and decided that the wisest thing of all would be to leave the carcass where it was – at least, for the time being.

McAnally figured one of his neighbors would finally put a name to the abomination that lay dead on his property, but nobody could offer one based only on his description. The next day someone loaned him a camera so that he could take a picture of the enigmatic beast. Devin duly snapped a couple of photos and then decided to bury its body in red clay about 10 feet from where it had been shot so that its remains could easily be located at a later date – if they were needed.

In the following weeks, McAnally spent quite a bit of time doing research in order to determine what kind of animal it was that had been killing his chickens and that now lay buried in his yard. He posted a photo of the creature up at famous De Leon's market, which he knew was frequented by some of the local old-timers. This action would prove profitable. One elderly woman who saw the picture commented that that the thing resembled the Chupacabras her grandmother had told her about back in Mexico when she was young. Similarly, an elderly man told how he had heard about a similar creature while growing up as a boy in Mexico during the 1930s, but it was known as the Chupasangre or blood-sucker. The creature had reportedly been blamed for the deaths of many small farm animals. Others suggested that the beast might be a stray Xolo, a hairless dog that is native to Mexico. A local hunting guide who examined the photo informed Devin that the animal was probably a muntjac, which is a type of small, Old World deer. The guide explained how muntjacs are frequently imported to Texas in order to be hunted as exotic game, and that the males can have long tusk-like canines. But, still, no-one could provide a definitive and satisfactory identification.

Devin thus began contacting various local media outlets, with the result being a flurry of news stories about the dead creature, which was now being labeled widely as a Chupacabras. And, at some point, the odd animal was memorably re-named the Elmendorf Beast. When the Beast's skull was eventually exhumed and taken to the San Antonio Zoo, a spokesperson could not conclusively identify what species it belonged to. Mammal curator John Gramieri stated that it might be a mix between a coyote and dog, but one with abnormal dentition and a skin condition known as sarcoptic mange which causes hair to fall out. Occasionally, dogs will scratch at their skin excessively causing their hide to become tough, rather like leather. Gramieri also noted that the skull possessed a very poor fusion in the jaw area, which seemed to allow its jaw to spread in an abnormal way, appearing more akin to the jaw of a reptile than that of a mammal. However, when a zoologist from the University of Texas was shown a photo of the skull, she quickly identified it as belonging to a coyote. Soon, Whitley Strieber took a keen interest and arranged to have DNA testing done. When the DNA results came back from the University of Cal-Davis genetics laboratory, Strieber confirmed that the Elmendorf Beast appeared to be some type of unusual coyote.

I've personally, and fortunately, had the opportunity to study the bones of the Elmendorf Beast on two separate occasions and I feel that they closely resemble those of a coyote, but with two significant exceptions. First, its canine teeth seem to be very exaggerated indeed, with the top and bottom teeth interlocking in a highly unusual manner. Also, the bony structure atop the skull, known as the sagittal crest, appears to be very pronounced indeed. This fact was later confirmed by veterinary expert Sharman Hoppes of Texas A&M University as part of the *Monster Quest* episode. However, Hoppes also stated that although the canines did appear somewhat exaggerated for a coyote, they weren't necessarily too long to belong to a domestic dog. All have agreed that the Beast's extreme lack of hair is highly unusual, and that if it is the result of mange, then it is one of the most extreme cases imaginable. Illuminating is the fact that no-one could explain its alleged vampire-like behavior.

A few months after the Elmendorf Beast made the headlines, another so-called Chupacabras was shot, at a place named Pollok, near the east Texas community of Lufkin. The memorable and monstrous events began one day during October of 2004 when the O'Quinn family heard

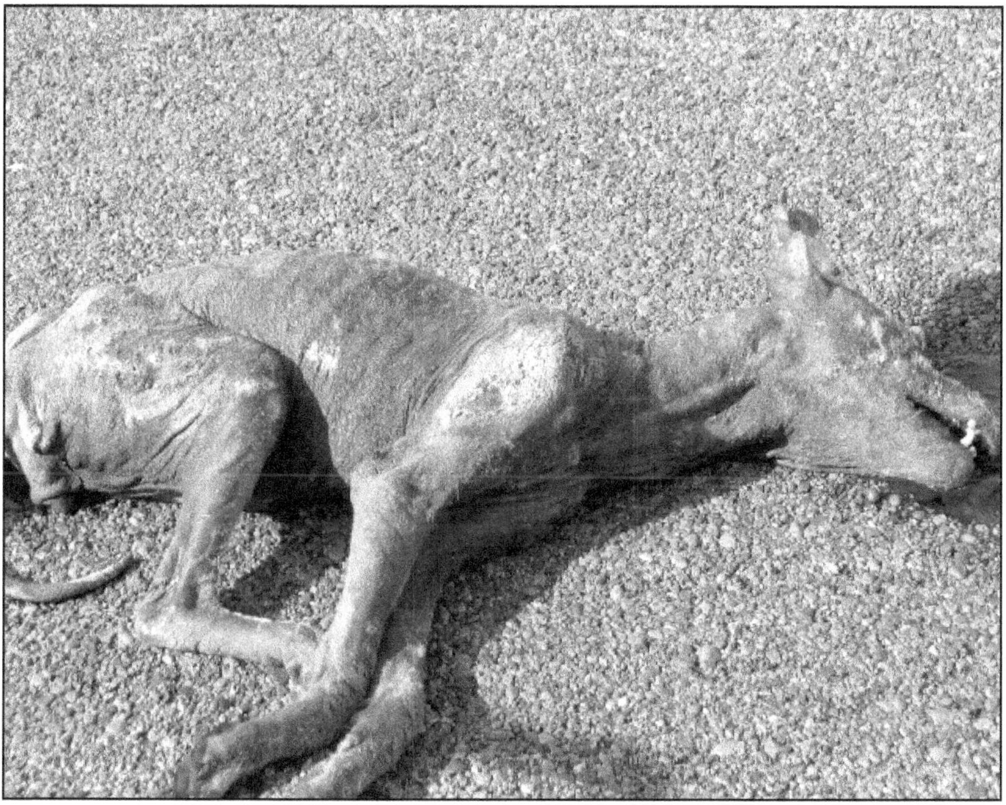

Above: Captured - the Fayetteville Chupacabras (Harvey Hayek)
Below: The Harvey Hayek Chupacabras Den (Ken Gerhard)

Above: The Hayek Chupacabra Gulley. (Ken Gerhard)
Below: The mounted specimen belonging to Dr Canion (CFZ)

their dogs carrying on outside their home. The large dogs had apparently cornered some kind of critter underneath the house and were whining in a distressed manner, but refused to go after whatever was causing their frenzy. Young Tyrel O'Quinn was instructed to crawl under the house with a rope and remove whatever was causing the disturbance. However, when he got within a few feet of the varmint, Tyrel became very upset by what he laid his eyes upon. The creature appeared to be a smoky, gray color, with long claws and very sharp teeth. It didn't look like anything he had ever seen, but seemed to resemble most all a gigantic monstrous rat. Subsequently, the frightening animal was shot by Tyrel's father Ben and finally dislodged. All who were present at the scene agreed that whatever the thing was, its appearance was truly horrific. The small monstrosity only weighed about 20 pounds and was virtually hairless, with necrotic skin, a severe overbite, grotesquely large fangs and a rat-like tail. Mystified, the O'Quinn family immediately called relative Stacy Womack, who worked at a local veterinary clinic to come and take a close look. On the way there, Womack spotted a very similar animal running across the road in front of her car. She later decided that, most probably, it was the mate of the dead creature.

When Stacy arrived at the scene, she inspected the carcass and took several photographs. She was perplexed as to precisely what she was looking at, since the specimen had a bluish color and forelimbs that appeared to be shorter than its rear limbs. In addition, the creature's claws and teeth appeared to be entirely too long and its body seemed to lack blood. When Stacy touched one of its ears she remembered that: "It broke off like a cookie." In the wake of the affair of the Elmendorf Beast, a great deal of publicity surrounded the Pollok Chupacabras. Once again, there was some disagreement as to what the animal might actually be. Local wildlife experts theorized that the specimen was most likely a mangy fox, or perhaps a coyote with certain genetic abnormalities.

A year later, during October of 2005, a third Chupacabras turned up in north-central Texas, this time on the outskirts of a community called Coleman. Like Devin McAnally, neighbors Reggie Lagow and Carol Burroughs began losing a significant number of chickens to an unknown culprit over a short period of time. Some of the chickens were missing, while others were found partially eaten, though there was usually little blood present. Lagow constructed a trap in an attempt to capture the crafty predator, but was unsuccessful. He was totally bewildered as to what he might be up against since the chicken thief seemed especially clever and hunted during the day, which was unlike foxes, skunks and other varmints he had previously dealt with. On one occasion, Reggie caught a fleeting glimpse of the creature running off with one of his chickens. He was unable to identify the animal, though it appeared to be of a strange, rusty color. When Lagow received word that one of his neighbors had successfully cornered and shot the beast in their chicken coop one day, he went over to see its body.

Carol Burroughs had also arrived at the scene and both she and Reggie took photographs of the weird animal which no-one present could identify. The creature was small, only about 13 pounds or so, and had a distinct blue color about it. It appeared to be covered in a light coat of wispy white hair that was similar to shorn lamb's wool. In addition, its muzzle appeared dog-like and it had big ears; its rear limbs looked abnormally long, and it possessed an exceptionally long tail. Unfortunately, due to the controversy that surrounded the shooting of a strangely out-of-place monkey near Lake Coleman a few years earlier, the body of the "Coleman Critter" was simply thrown in the trash. Like Devin McAnally, Reggie began to show a photo of the unidentified beast around town to see if anyone could put a name to it. First, he went to see veterinarian Johnny Needham, who worked right down the road from where he lived. Needham, who had lived in Conroe when the Pollok Chupacabras had been shot a year earlier, commented that the thing in the photo looked very similar to the other creature. As with the Elmendorf and Pollok creatures, the media quickly latched onto the story and news of the Coleman Chupacabras made the papers.

On a research trip in September of 2008, I decided to make a stop in Coleman, which lies approximately 50 miles to the south of Abilene. I wanted to gather any information I could on the Coleman Critter. I was able to reach Carol Burroughs by phone. The retired school-teacher told me in a cordial voice that the animal hadn't resembled anything else that she had ever seen before in her lifetime. Carol also remarked that the photos she had taken with her digital camera showed more detail than did the widely disseminated photo which Reggie Lagow had taken with his 35 millimeter. I also met with veterinarian Johnny Needham, who told me that the photos of the animal seemed perplexing to him when he first examined them. Needham was quite candid with me in expressing his view that the specimen was definitely not a coyote.

As I pulled into Reggie Lagow's driveway, the 92 year old was riding on his lawnmower. At first, he seemed slightly bewildered by the mysterious, black-clad man who was paying him a visit. However, once I had explained my purpose, he invited me inside to share his thoughts on the unusual creature. Reggie struck me as both worldly and wise, with an extremely pleasant disposition. He explained that he had lived in Coleman for more than a few years and had built his home with his own two hands. Before retirement, Lagow had worked for the military in aviation engineering, helping to assemble the great B-29 airplanes that helped to win the Second World War. Together, we carefully examined the most famous photo of the "critter", as Reggie called it, and we discussed what it might be. His biggest regret was that he had not preserved the body after the animal had been shot. But, at the time, all involved parties were concerned about a possible backlash from animal rights activists. Reggie told me that the creature was, in his opinion, the result of some type of medical experiment: "Of two different kinds of flesh," as he memorably put it. He confessed that similar beasts had been seen since by other Coleman residents, though none of them wanted to go on the record.

During the summer of 2007, the biggest hoopla involving a Texas Chupacabras took place near the southern town of Cuero, which lies just north-west of Victoria, in DeWitt County. Local rancher Dr. Phylis Canion took keen notice when six kittens disappeared off her property over a short time period. Before too long, she also discovered several of her chickens dead in their coop. Their blood had been completely drained. Phylis at first thought that the perpetrator might be a bobcat, and she did in fact shoot a large one around that time. But the killings quickly resumed. Soon, she and her husband, Steve, began having sightings of a strange animal on their land. Phylis, a published author who works in the medical field as a nutritional expert, is no stranger to animals, having been raised in the great outdoors of Texas. In addition, she lived in Africa for a number of years, where she participated in safaris and hunted big game with Steve, an oil worker. While in Africa, the couple was able to observe many diverse and exotic species in their natural habitat. But the creature that was lurking on their property seemed unnatural to both of them in many ways. For example, the animal was usually seen during the day and did not seem at all intimidated by their presence – very unlike coyotes they had encountered. Also, the thing seemed to run in a highly unusual manner. And something about its skin looked abnormal too.

Phylis mentioned the mysterious events to her neighbors and was duly rewarded one morning when she received a call, alerting her to an unusual road-kill on the highway near her ranch. The resourceful rancher drove over and collected the dead animal with her front loader and then laid it out on a burlap feed-sack snapping several photos.

As with the other creatures, the Cuero Chupacabras was virtually hairless, except for a wisp of dark hair running the length of its back. Its purple skin was wrinkled like an elephant's and it possessed ghoulishly long fans, though curiously, it was completely missing all of its front incisor teeth. In addition, the animal had sharp claws, and its rear limbs seemed elongated. Despite being struck by a car, there was very little blood present on the carcass. Unlike the other creatures, this was an impressively substantial beast, weighing at least 40 pounds, and much larger than the coyotes that typically roam the south Texas plains. Within four days of recovering the body, Phylis received word that some neighbors had found two similar animals dead on their land. There had, in fact, been a lot of rain in the area at the time and the creek bottoms were flooding. She thought that perhaps the bad weather might have forced the creatures out of their hiding place in the bottoms and onto the high roads.

What happened next was sensational. Phyllis removed the skin and head of the animal and preserved the flesh by freezing it, in order to facilitate possible DNA testing. Media outlets from around the world caught wind and descended on her property in order to film Phylis displaying the controversial remains. San Antonio reporter Joe Conger arranged for a tissue sample to be analyzed at Texas State University by biology professor, Dr. Mike Forster. A couple of weeks later, Forster announced that genetics indicated that the mysterious creature was merely a coyote. But, by that time, news of Phylis and her frozen Chupacabras head were making headlines worldwide, from the United States, to Italy, to Japan. Phyllis even had some commemorative t-shirts made, which featured an artist's interpretation of the beast, along with the slogan "*2007 The Year of the Chupacabras*". To her surprise, she ultimately sold thousands of the inexpensive shirts to curious people all around the globe.

My involvement with the Cuero case began in February of 2008, during my work for the television series *Monster Quest*. Phylis had told producer Joe Schneier that she had seen a Chupacabras creature prowling her property in recent weeks, so we mutually decided to plan an expedition there in order to try to capture the thing alive, or to at least to try and get it on film. My good friend, naturalist Lee Hales of Slidell, Louisiana agreed to join the hunt. Lee, who shares an interest in mysterious animals, had accompanied me on research projects before and, on this one, would assist me in setting out various baits and traps in hopes of drawing the critter out of its hiding place.

Prior to filming, I took a preliminary trip down to the Canion Ranch, in order to have a private viewing of the frozen remains. I also wanted to interview the Canions and assess the terrain of their property. Phylis and Steve immediately struck me as extremely gracious and down-to-earth people. The walls of their beautiful, ranch style home were adorned with mounts of zebras, antelopes and other exotic game that they had bagged in Africa. Phylis told me that she had been a hunter her whole life. She knew her animals. We chatted for a half-hour as we toured the property, and then Phylis finally brought out the smelly, thawed Chupacabras head so that I could examine it. My first impression was that its skull seemed quite broad and square, not at all like the familiar streamlined head of a coyote. Its teeth struck me as most unusual, with grossly exaggerated canine fangs. Its incisor teeth were completely absent. Upon closer inspection of its hide, I could see that there were a few very sparse hairs present, but the animal's dark skin basically looked bare and wrinkled like leather. I took several photographs and measurements of the specimen, and then phoned Joe Schneier with my observations.

For the *Monster Quest* episode, Lee and I laid out plenty of raw meat and blood in strategic locations around the Canion property, including the chicken coop where many chickens had been found dead. We also set out a steel trap and placed a live chicken in a cage next to it. In addition, we doused the area with coyote urine, in hopes that we might draw in any predators that were in the area. The producers supplied us with several motion-activated cameras and an advanced call-blast system, loaded with recordings of distressed animals, all of which were put to very good use. Despite a few tantalizing moments, ultimately we didn't catch our quarry, only a large, cranky possum that had the bad luck to stumble into our trap. But, after filming had wrapped-up for the evening, Phylis drew our attention to some high-pitched barking sounds that were emanating from the thick brush nearby. We all listened very intently for several minutes and were in agreement that whatever it was, it sounded like a small domestic dog, as opposed to a coyote. Eventually, two lower pitched barks answered back and then there was silence. The next morning, after the television crew had departed, I investigated the location where we had heard the barking noises and discovered a network of well-worn game trails and some suspicious looking burrows or dens.

When the Chupacabras episode of *Monster Quest* aired on the History Channel during November of 2008, the results of the new DNA tests were revealed. They indicated that the Cuero Chupacabras was most likely a mix between a coyote and a wolf, despite the fact that wolves are largely presumed extinct in Texas. The Elmendorf Beast results indicated it was probably a hybrid of a domestic dog and a coyote. No clear answers were available as to why these animals were virtually hairless. Without live tissue to work with, the mange theory could not be proven. Just weeks after the filming of the episode had wrapped, Phylis apparently found the carcass of a second, smaller creature on her neighbor's property. This one was scrawny and emaciated with long fangs, razor-sharp claws and cloudy, blue, eyes. Like the others, it looked sickly and hairless, with a bizarre skin condition.

Then on August 8, a deputy sheriff near Cuero captured video of a live Chupacabras on his dashboard camera. Deputy Brandon Reidell of DeWitt County was patrolling fence-lines, when the hairless animal emerged from some brush and ran in front of his patrol car for a couple of minutes. Reidell instinctively switched on his camera and filmed the thing trotting along, with the resulting footage being picked up by CNN and broadcast nationwide. The footage shows a creature that resembles a canine, except that it appears to be hairless. It trots along in front of Reidell's patrol car for several paces and at one point even turns its head, revealing what appears to be a long, pig-like snout. Skeptics have written off this aspect of the video as an optical illusion, created by the angle of the camera lens through the windshield. But others that have watched the video are drawn to this strange characteristic. When asked about the incident, Deputy Reidell confessed that he had never seen anything like the creature before, and added that the thing did not seem to run like any of the coyotes he'd seen, due to the fact that its rear legs appeared longer than its front two.

De Witt County appears to be a prime breeding ground for the Texas Chupacabras, because within weeks of Reidell's video, specifically on August 30, two more creatures were apparently shot by mechanic Paul Jones on his property near Terryville. Jones' grandfather had been the first to spot one beast weeks earlier, and when family friend Brian Wilborn encountered it again while clearing some brush, a careful search was quickly mounted. The result being that Jones was able to nab one of the critters in the afternoon and another one just a few hours later in the same vicinity. The beasts were examined by several men who were present and they could only agree that the creatures resembled mangy coyotes, as well as the Chupacabras beasts in the photos that they had seen on television. Oilfield worker Jason Marburn commented: "It doesn't look like any coyote or mixed breed I have ever seen. It looks like it ain't from around here."

Following a lecture that Nick Redfern was giving to a group of San Antonio UFO researchers during November of 2008, legendary UFO researcher and Schertz native Walt Andrus produced a skull that he explained was from yet another Chupacabras. According to Andrus, it had been given to him by an associate, who had shot the animal somewhere near Elmendorf. The skull closely resembled that of the Elmendorf Beast, with the same, pronounced sagital crest. However, the teeth appeared to be completely normal in appearance and lacking in the abnormalities that I had observed in the other animals. Several months later, Andrus mailed the skull to Nick, who, in October 2009, was filmed by a team from the National Geographic Channel who were in the process of making a documentary on the Chupacabras – of both Texas and Puerto Rico.

Taking into account the fact that additional so-called Chupacabras creatures have been reported at other places around Texas in recent months, it would seem that there is a sort of population explosion taking place with these things, whatever they may be.

This is evidenced by the events on the Hayek property near Fayetteville, where several family members have apparently had sightings of animals that they say closely resemble Chupacabras. The family's patriarch Harvey Hayek got in touch with me after contacting Phyllis Canion. During our initial phone conversation, Harvey explained to me how he'd first come across one of the creatures while clearing brush during the summer of 2007. The animal did not seem at all intimidated by Hayek as he rode on his tractor. In fact, it circled around him several times, as if to size him up. Soon after that incident, Hayek's son, Derek, took a rifle-shot at one of the varmints by a gulley. Derek thought he had hit his mark when the thing went down momentarily, but then it got up and ran away. On another occasion, as Harvey was shredding brush on his property, he flushed out several of the beasts all at once, causing the group to flee to the nearby Colorado River. In the spot where the creatures had emerged from, the family found flattened grass that looked like it could have acted as a large bedding area. On yet another occasion, Harvey and his wife spotted one of the odd-looking creatures lurking by the gulley one day and watched it for several minutes as it sat leisurely behind a bush, nonchalantly staring back at them.

Rural Fayetteville is located halfway between Houston and Austin near the Colorado River. When I drove out to the Hayek residence one weekend to conduct an investigation, the entire Hayek clan heartily welcomed me and immediately made me feel right at home. All of those present were in firm agreement that there were indeed mysterious creatures roaming their property. Their descriptions were very familiar: the beasts were weird hairless varmints that seemed to hop around like kangaroos. Several of us drove out to the gulley where most of the sightings had taken place and I was shown a series of large burrows that peppered the red clay and the cliff walls surrounding it. Upon close inspection, I concluded that the burrows most definitely were animal dens of some kind, perhaps an expansive network even, and one that extended deep into the cliff walls. I was amused when Harvey stated the obvious and suggested that I poke a very long stick down into one of them in order to see if anything happened. Being that my profession frequently warrants such potentially-hazardous actions, I carefully followed his suggestion, unfortunately with no result. We agreed that the best plan of action would be to try and trap one of these animals alive, if possible, something which has never been done successfully. Within a few months, a television documentary for the National Geographic Channel would provide us with an opportunity to try. With the Hayek's cooperation, we mounted an expedition on their property

That particular venture took place during June of 2009 and involved some new tools, including a thermal imaging viewer, as well as a tranquilizer rifle provided by a local veterinarian. Though we did not locate our prey that evening, Harvey caught wind of a road-killed animal near Fayetteville that fitted the descriptions of what he'd observed on his property. He had the good sense of mind to find out where the carcass had been buried and dug up its remains. When we examined it for the National Geographic film crew, the smelly remains had all the earmarks of the other Texas Chupacabras creatures. The producers sent the specimen up to Texas Tech University for further evaluation.

In March of 2008, I received a call from a man named Greg Davis who told me that he had just videotaped a Chupacabras on the far west side of San Antonio, which is only a mere dozen miles from my home! When I visited the Davis residence in order to examine the footage with Greg and his wife, I witnessed a now very familiar sight: essentially, a weird, hairless canine similar in build to a coyote. The animal was sitting calmly on a paved lot near a wooded area. It got up after a moment or so and trotted off into the brush. Strangely enough, the location of Greg's sighting was in a heavily populated suburban area surrounding Leon Creek. A few days after his first encounter, Davis saw the creature again – in the same spot – and watched as a neighborhood woman attempted to give the skittish Chupacabras some water and a bowl of dog food! However, her actions only resulted in the animal dashing across the street into a nearby sub-division, which is apparently the last time it was ever seen. As I prepared to leave the Davis residence, Greg presented me with two zip lock bags. One contained droppings he had collected at the location. The other held a cat's severed limb that he had found amidst a pile of fur, apparently the only remains of a Chupacabras attack.

So where does that leave us, after all the publicity and analysis that has resulted from the appearance of these ghoulish canines? People often ask me: are the Texas Chupacabras merely mangy coyotes? To simply say "yes", I personally feel, is an over-simplification. Examination of their physical remains, DNA tests and analysis, has confirmed that these animals belong to the genus Canis. It's also true that the closest genetic matches have been with coyotes, though both the Elmendorf Beast and Cuero Chupacabras may have been hybrids. It seems plausible to theorize that an extreme type of mange is being passed from mothers to their offspring, causing their hairless condition. My associate, naturalist Lee Hales has pointed out that adaptations happen all of the time in nature, and maybe their baldness has even given them an advantage on the hot plains of Texas. Perhaps it is even being written into their genetic code.

But, as of yet, no-one has been able to sufficiently explain their other abnormal characteristics, which have included grossly, enlarged fangs and claws, irregular skulls, disproportionate limbs and unusually long tails. These are all traits that seem inexplicable. Phylis Canion has also suggested that these creatures might possess cataracts in their eyes, resulting in poor vision. This would certainly explain why so many of them have been shot so easily or run over by cars. There is also the issue of their sinister behavior, which seemingly revolves around lapping up the blood of helpless poultry. Some people in the medical field, including Phylis, have pointed out that there could be specific nutrients in blood that these animals crave, due to their affliction. Still, exactly what are these blue zombie dogs that roam the grasslands of Texas?

Perhaps Reggie Lagow was accurate in his muse that the Chupacabras could be part of some vast conspiracy involving genetic manipulation by sinister forces like the military, secret organizations or even aliens. Or, maybe we are witnessing the signs of man's impact on the environment. It could be that our wastefulness is causing mutations or diseases we have not seen before. Either way, it has become clearly evident that the Texas Chupacabras, whatever they may be, are breeding.

Breaking News!
In August of 2009, another so-called Chupacabras carcass turned up at a taxidermy school in Blanco, Texas. The school's owner, Jerry Ayer, obtained the carcass from one of his students, who had poisoned the strange creature in a barn near the town of Rosenberg. Ayer noted that the animal was unlike anything he had ever seen before: completely hairless, with gray, leathery skin and forelimbs that were longer than its rear limbs. Ultimately, Mr. Ayer mounted the specimen and sold it to *The Lost Museum*. Tissue samples were taken by CFZ investigators Richie and Naomi West, and at the time of going to press we are still awaiting the results of the DNA tests.

Still from *Wild Man of the Navidad* (Greeks Productions, Inc.)

Chapter IV
The Navidad Wild Man
(Nick Redfern)

It was a truly horrific and nightmarish beast that provoked both overwhelming fear and intense alarm within the minds and hearts of the fine folk that lived in the small and somewhat isolated Texan town of Sublime throughout the 1830s. It roamed the dense and mysterious thickets and fields of an area whose people became terrified of the unknown entity in their midst. And it rapidly became known to those that were forced to live in its dark shadow by the memorable moniker of the Wild Man of the Navidad.

So the notable legend goes, at the turn of the 1830s, strange and hard-to-identify barefoot tracks of two so-called "wild people" were often found both in and around the varied settlements of Texas's lower Navidad, specifically in the area of Sublime which can be found roughly halfway between the cities of San Antonio and Houston. Generally speaking the tracks were relatively small, and much consideration was given to the possibility that there was both a male and a female on the loose. Keen and alert guard dogs on local ranches and properties would on occasion react both violently and furiously when the strange and unidentified visitors were believed to be quietly and carefully prowling throughout the area late after nightfall had enveloped the entire area. And there were even reports of the mysterious pair breaking into people's homes and stealing food.

According to the legends and tales that inevitably surfaced in the wake of the initial wave of mysterious reports and encounters, a human skeleton was later discovered in the area – something that led a number of commentators to conclude that the wild woman's larger, male companion had possibly died. Precisely what happened to the skeleton – if indeed it ever really existed, of course – remains unknown and is unfortunately lost to the inevitable fog of time.

An initial attempt, organized by a group of men in the area, to hunt down the other mysterious hairy hominid utterly failed. On the second occasion, however, there was an intriguing development in this early somewhat Bigfoot-like affair.

As inevitably is the case in campfire style tales such as this one, it was a distinctly dark and stormy night, and a shadowy, monstrous and mighty form loomed perilously into view. Whatever he, she or it was, the unidentified visitor was relatively slim and unclothed, but was curiously and notably described as having a body that was covered – head to toe – in short brown hair. The brave band of men valiantly tried to seize the beast; however, it skillfully bounded out of the area with what was later described as truly astonishing speed.

The odd event remained utterly unresolved until a group of locals allegedly cornered a runaway male slave in the same area. This latest development in the strange saga seemingly satisfied local newspaper editors, who unanimously concluded that the wild man and woman of the Navidad were actually nothing of the sort at all. In reality, the media grandly asserted, the tales were merely based upon nothing stranger than misidentifications of the aforementioned unfortunate slave – who had presumably escaped from his "masters" and who had been trying to survive in the harsh wilds of the Navidad for years.

Taking into careful consideration the fact that certainly not everyone was in agreement with that particularly down-to-earth conclusion, however, yet another valiant attempt was initiated to try and resolve the mystery of the unknown entities and their identities, this time once and for all. A team of experienced hunters from Sublime decided that a complete check of the nearby thick atmospheric woods was the only real viable option left available to them, if matters were ever to be firmly laid to rest.

After several fruitless searches, the group well and truly hit the absolute jackpot when one of them reported seeing what looked to be a wild-looking human being racing along an adjacent prairie. Men with lassos urgently pursued their quarry, while others with dogs ensured that there was no chance at all of it escaping into the heart of the dense woodland. Nevertheless, and initially at least, the hunters were wholly outwitted by the hairy man-thing. It was destined not to remain missing for too long however.

Under a bright, moonlit sky of a type that would be very welcome in any self respecting horror movie, the heart-thumping excitement of the previous several hours was finally beginning to subside, when the hounds suddenly became agitated and nervous. Not only that: something, or someone, was loudly crashing through the thick bushes – and in the specific direction of the hunters, no less. The creature suddenly appeared again, bounded across the prairie, and raced for the protection and cover of the dense forest. Whatever it was, this was most certainly no normal human being. Indeed, the nearest hunter reported that his horse was so afraid that it refused to go anywhere near the hairy monstrosity.

By this time, the wild thing was coming perilously close to the forest, and the lead hunter realized that it was quite literally a case of now or never. He excitedly spurred his horse on and threw his lasso. Unfortunately, it missed its target and the beast made good its escape, deep into the heart of the darkened forest. Although the attempted capture of the monster of the Navidad had ended in complete failure, one important point should not go without observation or comment. The hunter in question had an excellent opportunity to note the physical appearance of the creature as both he and it charged wildly across the open prairie. Precisely like others who had come before him, the hunter described the man-thing as being naked, with bright staring eyes and a body covered in short, brown hair. It was also said to be carrying something in its hand. Very interestingly, nothing less than a five foot long, carefully fashioned wooden club was reportedly later found in the same area where the furious and famous pursuit had taken place. And thus was born the dark and unforgettable legend of the Wild Man of the Navidad.

Over the years and decades that followed, the story and legend of Sublime's Wild Man surfaced occasionally in books, magazines and periodicals – and certainly most prominently of all within the pages of J. Frank Dobie's 1938 book, *Tales of Old-Time Texas*, which was published by the Texas Folklore Society. Now, more than 70 years after Dobie's book first surfaced, the Wild Man of the Navidad has made a bold and dramatic return – in a new film – courtesy of an Austin, Texas-based film company called Greeks Productions, and Kim Henkel, the writer of one of the most notorious and revered horror films of all time, *The Texas Chainsaw Massacre*.

Greeks Productions is the brainchild of 30-something filmmakers Justin Meeks and Duane Graves. Meeks grew up in the Texan city of Corpus Christi, and received degrees in psychology and film at Texas A&M University in 2001, before moving to Austin and landing a role on the television show *Prison Break*. Graves was born and raised in San Antonio and, like Meeks, also secured a degree in film at Texas A&M, and went on to direct the critically acclaimed documentary *Up Syndrome*, an intimate portrait of a childhood friend born with Down's Syndrome.

Kim Henkel had been the pair's Professor of Screenwriting and Film Production at Texas A&M, something that provided both Meeks and Graves with the perfect background and opportunity to immerse themselves in the world of on-screen terror. And so, upon setting up Greeks Productions, in the spring of 2002 the duo quickly set to work on a trilogy of short, black and white, 16mm horror films: *Headcheese* (described by *Shock Cinema* magazine as having the "gritty backwoods atmosphere of some lost grind-house classic") *Voltagen* and *The Hypostatic Union*, all of which were released internationally by Shock-O-Rama Cinema.

But what was it that prompted the pair to develop the strange story of the Wild Man of the Navidad for the big screen? When I heard about the movie, I contacted Duane Graves, who told me: "We knew we wanted to do a horror movie set in Texas, but we didn't really have a story. I had heard of the Wild Man – kind of like a handed-down story from my grandfather. But I didn't know too much about it. So, we started reading up on old Texas legends, got a copy of J. Frank Dobie's *Tales of Old-Time Texas* and read about the Wild Man of the Navidad. Then we went to Sublime to check the place out."

Graves continued: "We went there on a kind of production scouting trip. The idea was to stick to the conventional story that everyone had written about. While we were there, we would go in this little place called Red's Tavern, which is really the only place in town, and talk to the old folks about the Wild Man, and it was through them that we got hooked up with a guy named Dale S. Rogers."

It transpired that Rogers was related to a certain Reverend Samuel Rogers, on whose land many of the original Wild Man of the Navidad encounters had occurred way back in the 1800s. Over the years, the reverend had carefully collected numerous jaw-dropping stories pertaining to sightings of the beast and its ghastly activities, many of which were published in J. Frank Dobie's *Tales of Old-Time Texas*. As they delved further into the mystery, Graves and Meeks learned that until the mid 1970s, Dale S. Rogers and his invalided wife had lived in a quaint ranch house that was situated on the very same Texas acreage that the long dead reverend had previously owned, a great deal of which is heavily wooded, and reputedly still unexplored to any meaningful degree to this very day.

Presently, a Texas Historical Marker detailing the legend of The Wild Man of the Navidad can be found on the perimeter of the Rogers' land, which sits alongside Highway 90, west of Sublime. Even now, travelers visiting the marker report hearing unusual and bone-chilling "bellowing sounds" from deep within the woods that surround the Navidad River and that extend beyond the lonely stretch of highway.

Recently retired, Rogers has now begun to talk about his own sightings of the Wild Man – or more likely a descendent, or descendents, of the original beasts – that occurred as late as 1975. Indeed, Rogers told Graves and Meeks that: "All of these ideas of the Wild Man being some sort of slave [are] a bunch of fabricated baloney. Those things were out there for years and they still might be. I saw one many times. My daddy saw it. My granddaddy saw it. It was more animal than anything else. And if anyone crossed it, it sure wouldn't hesitate to let you know that."

Gaining Rogers' trust, Graves and Meeks were provided with his detailed and absolutely indispensable journals that carefully chronicled and described the many and varied historic Wild Man encounters in the vicinity, as well as old Super-8 films of the area, and illustrations of the creature – all of which, collectively, became the firm inspiration for the movie.

Graves added that: "We then hooked up with Ken, as he'd been our professor in college and had written *Chainsaw*. He came on-board, and Justin and me started developing it, as co-writers and directors. Everyone kept telling us we should make it into a slasher movie, killing teenagers. We didn't want that. We wanted to keep it as close to the original legend and [to] Dale's journals as we could."

The movie will not disappoint those with a deep passion for horror, cryptozoology and Forteana: it is darkly rich in atmosphere, and conjures up graphic and unsettling imagery of a sinister little town that is sitting atop a wealth of eerie and ominous secrets. And to describe the locale as a little town is not an exaggeration; by 2000, the population of Sublime had only reached 75. Try and imagine the best parts of *Twin Peaks*, *The X Files* and *The Legend of*

Courtesy IFC Films / Greeks Productions, Inc

Still from *Wild Man of the Navidad* (Greeks Productions, Inc.)

Boggy Creek thrown into the mix, and then given a strong shot of independent film making of a distinctly cool kind, and you have *The Wild Man of the Navidad*. Graves concluded to me: "It's been a long process – about two years – but we're pleased how it turned out. We've only recently completed it. It's had two public screenings, one of which was at the campus where we went to school. We had a real good turn out and the reaction was great. Everyone seemed to really get it and appreciate it for what it was. We think it works. We'd love to get a theatrical release, and then we'll hopefully go after a DVD release too. But the next thing for us is to hit the major film festivals: that's where the magic happens."

Before we move on to pastures new and different, it's worth mentioning that other apparent wild men have been reported throughout the Lone Star State. In other words, the Wild Man – and Woman – of the Navidad were not alone. As evidence of this, on March 22, 1892, the *Galveston Daily News* newspaper reported the following story that originated in San Antonio:

"Mr. George Cole and Jimmie Hightower returned Thursday from a ten day fish and hunt in the bottoms of the San Antonio River in Refugle County, about 40 miles from Golind. Mr. Coles relates an adventure which he had while gone with a wild man of the forest.

"'We saw coming towards us on the opposite side of the river, what appeared to be a man of about 60 years of age. His beard and hair were long and wavy and he was almost entirely nude, his only articles of clothing being sandals upon his feet and a turban-like hat upon his head. His body was covered with a thick growth of black, shaggy hair. He walked erect with his arms folded upon his breast, and came within 60 or 100 yards of us. Our presence did not seem to startle him in the least. I called to him in English, Spanish, and French, but he paid no attention whatsoever and calmly continued his walk up the river bank.'

"Mr. Cole remained near this spot for several days, but saw no more of this strange being. A party should be organized to go for this wild man of the woods about April 1."

Consider, too, this story from the *Dallas Morning News* of March 31, 1901 which surfaced in the area of Santo: "There is much excitement near Judd Switch because of a negro who seems to be wild and insane. He has been in the neighborhood about two months. About twenty men gathered in the John Morris neighborhood last night and tried to capture him. They found where he had built a fire, but he was not there, and they made a drive for him with hounds, but could not catch him. He can run like a pony. He is perfectly nude, except for something around his waist that reaches down about half way of his things. The people tomorrow will make another effort to catch him."

Similarly, there is an account from the *Galveston Daily News* of June 26, 1908: "A supposed wild man is creating consternation in the Charles Steelhammer neighborhood. He visits houses at night or while the families are away and helps himself to whatever his fancy craves. He laps up the cream like a dog and eats fried chicken raw, so they say.

A number of citizens of that community sleep in arms and carry their scatter guns and forty-some-odds in their work for fear of being chewed up by this great human monstrosity. He has been seen a number of times, and each time those who saw him describe his manner of running as resembling the lope of a wolf, and not unlike the flight of an airship. Well, do not be hard on the poor, frenzied, half-famished creature; he is probably some eminent Republican who ran away to keep from being nominated for the vice presidency."

Chapter V
Trailing the Texan Bigfoot
(Ken Gerhard)

While the vast majority of all Bigfoot reports in Texas stem from the thick swampy bottom-lands that comprise the eastern third of the state, there are a number of well-documented sightings that have emanated from deep within the heartland, and even amid the barren scrublands that surround El Paso to the west. Some of the earliest accounts appear in the classic book, *Sasquatch: The Apes Among Us*, written by Canadian researcher John Green, who has spent decades dedicatedly collecting and analyzing countless reports of hairy man-giants from all over North America. Green dedicated several pages to Texas sightings in his impressive compilation, published in 1978.

Without a doubt, the most notable events occurred during July of 1969, when a creature known as the Lake Worth Monster appeared before dozens of eyewitnesses at the Greer Island Nature Center on the outskirts of Fort Worth. Initially the monster was described as resembling a scale-covered Goat Man of sorts. But later on, witnesses compared the thing to an enormous white-colored ape or a Bigfoot-type creature. Since we have done a great deal of research on Lake Worth's Goat Man, Nick Redfern has highlighted the exploits of that particular creature in its own chapter of this book, leaving us to explore other man-beasts from around the state in this particular section of *Monsters of Texas*.

There have been a smattering of Bigfoot reports from the Texas hill country, particularly the region around Lake Travis, near Austin. There also exists a dubious story about a hirsute, feral boy that was supposedly captured near Austin back in 1875. In addition, on the outskirts of San Antonio to the south, a man named John Martinez and his friend Rick were rabbit hunting during November of 1974, when they reported seeing a six or seven foot tall creature with long matted hair on its head. Their dog even snarled at the menacing monster.

A letter that the late anthropologist and Bigfoot researcher Dr. Grover Krantz received during 1975 described a sighting which took place about 30 miles north of San Antonio at a private lake. The letter writer explained how the eyewitness had been fishing at the small secluded body of water on a 20,000 acre property when he heard a loud splash. Gazing across the water, the man observed a large, gray figure standing on top of a 150 foot high limestone cliff opposite him. Since he could not make out much in the way of details, the man relied on the scope of a rifle he was carrying in order to observe the creature more clearly. As he did so, the witness was able to estimate that the animal stood eight or nine feet tall and he could tell it had long gray fur and a round, cat-like head. He watched the thing evidently manhandling some large branches for about five minutes or so. The following morning, the curious man made his way over to the spot where the huge figure had been standing and observed trampled brush, broken branches and a massive, overturned boulder.

A military base in a major city is probably the very last place from where you would ever expect to hear Bigfoot reports emanating, but nonetheless, there was an intriguing spate of such sightings near San Antonio's now defunct Kelly Air Force Base during the summer of 1976. It all began when 28 year old Ed Olivarri, at the time a telephone worker living near the corner of West Fenfield and Quintana Roads, noticed that his small black dog, Lickem, was barking at something in the yard at around seven in the morning. Ed went outside to try and see what the commotion was all about. Because his view was obstructed by a neighbor's tool shed, Olivarri proceeded cautiously and carefully to the picket fence that ran along an alley behind his house. From there, he could make out the figure of a large animal lying on the ground with its back to him, and at a distance of about 40 yards. When a train whistle sounded from nearby railroad tracks, he watched in disbelief as a seven foot tall brown hairy creature stood up on two legs and ran off like a man into close by woods. Ed was unsurprisingly hesitant to tell anyone about what he had seen, for fear of frightening his elderly mother, Guadalupe, but eventually confided in his brother about the strange visitor.

A few nights after his first sighting, Ed was returning from a bar at around 2.00 a.m., when he noticed a figure with green, glowing eyes standing by a doghouse in his yard. At first he paid no notice to the mysterious visitor. But later, as Ed lay in bed, it occurred to him that the figure had been far too tall to be a dog. For weeks following Olivarri's sightings, the neighborhood dogs began howling and carrying on throughout the night, while the cats seemed to prefer the safety of the rooftops. Ed's 20 year old sister, Yolanda, even discovered a mangled cat in their back yard. Its head had been twisted around in a grotesque and horrific fashion.

Another major incident occurred on August 30, when the Olivarri's next-door neighbor Rose Medina was awakened by her dog barking at around three in the morning. Looking out of her window, Rose observed a furry light brown-colored animal sitting on her back step. She was able to get a good look at the thing, since there was a security light in the backyard and Rose decided that the creature looked distinctly ape-like and was about the size of a nine year old child. A terrified Mrs. Medina tapped on the glass in attempt to frighten the being away. It finally ran off when another one of the house's occupants opened a window. Rose later estimated that the tiny, man-like animal stood about three feet tall.

Upon hearing about Mrs. Medina's encounter, Ed Olivarri deduced that there likely had to be a female Bigfoot and her offspring living in the nearby woods. He duly searched the surrounding area and discovered some large, footprint-shaped impressions situated near a creek bed. Local reporters, who had shown up to cover the story, carefully inspected the tracks. A game warden also came out to investigate, but by then the prints had been trampled over by curious neighbors and the warden left the scene completely baffled.

There was also a mystery which surrounded a heavy manhole cover near the Olivarri's backyard. One night it had been lifted from its resting place by some unknown force, the opening exposing running water below. There was also a 14 inch long, man-like footprint found next to the manhole. No utility workers had been seen around that time and the object weighed several hundred pounds; in other words, it was far too heavy to have been moved easily. Moreover, neighbors began to recall a grisly unexplained murder, years earlier that had involved a teenage girl who had apparently been found with a tree branch impaled through her body.

Meanwhile, one of Ed Olivarri's aunts heard of an intriguing story from a woman that she had met at the local Laundromat. The woman evidently was not aware of the Bigfoot sightings that had taken place. She had told the aunt that a gentleman friend of hers had been walking home near Dwight Jr. High School on Southcross Street around 10:30 one night, when he heard something coming out of the brush right behind him. As the man turned around, he was shocked to the core to see a tall hairy man-like creature staring at him. The distraught witness broke into a run, but to his horror the being then began to give chase. Only when the man called out to some young people for help, did his pursuer fall behind and finally vanish from sight. For the rest of that strange summer, the neighborhood was abuzz with curiosity seekers, including a self-proclaimed UFO researcher, whilst the local police were forced to patrol the area on an increased basis as a direct result of all the commotion. After a while, however, and chiefly because there were no further reports, the hysteria around Quintana Road ended.

Being a resident of San Antonio, I couldn't wait to investigate the neighborhood where the sightings had taken place. When I spoke to the family that now occupies the house where Ed Olivarri had lived at the time of the incidents, they were totally unaware of the events that had transpired there years earlier, and probably thought that I was completely out of my mind. But, the eldest son Ramiro was gracious enough to give me a tour of the property and together we located the infamous manhole cover.

Other neighbors that I spoke with remembered Rose Medina and also that the neighborhood was at one time surrounded by thick brushy woods, which had then just recently been cleared away. There are, in fact, some small tracts of brush that still remain next to Quintana Road. What many people fail to realize, is that San Antonio, despite its large population, is very much a frontier city on the edge of an enormous expanse of very wild habitat. Therefore, it's not at all unusual to see deer and other wild animals running through the city's suburban neighborhoods. And, it's important to note that Kelly Air Force Base itself, which is now closed, was at one time comprised of hundreds of acres of forestland.

Another notable Bigfoot incident from the 1970s which made Texas headlines involved a monster that became known as the Hawley Him. So the story goes, at 10 in the morning of July 6, 1977, two youths from the Abilene Boy's Ranch, 14 year old Tom Roberts and 15 year old Larry Suggs were clearing brush on Bob Scott's land near Hawley, just north of Abilene. While they were taking a break in the hot sun, the teens both noticed a rotten smell. A few moments later they were startled by the sounds of tree limbs breaking and suddenly found themselves the target of a shower of good-sized rocks. One rock actually struck Larry in the right calf creating a bruise, while another projectile barely and luckily missed his head.

When they turned to see their attacker, the youths were confronted by what was described as: "A shaggy seven foot monster with long, dangling arms." Larry later recalled that: "It was kind of an ape, but still a man. He had huge arms. They hung to his knees. You'd have to see it to believe it." The bizarre creature didn't make a sound, other than the snapping of brush as it moved around. Understandably, the boys abandoned their tools and headed for the safety of a neighbor's house, occasionally catching glimpses of the thing as they fled.

When they arrived at the McFarland residence, Tom and Larry were visibly upset and shaken. The boys did eventually return to the site of the attack, but only when they were accompanied by 13 year old Renee McFarland, who wisely brought along a 30/30 rifle for good measure. When the trio arrived at the scene, they immediately spotted the monster lurking in some brush. A nervous Renee apparently handed the rifle to Larry with instructions to quickly shoot the beast. He somehow managed to gather up his nerve and fire at the creature, with the resulting recoil of the weapon knocking him to the ground. None of the teens were sure if he'd hit his mark, but the target did take off in a hurry, crashing through some thick foliage as it did so.

Upon an investigation of the scene, Tom and Larry discovered a track which, they felt, had been left by the creature. When the police arrived at the scene, Renee revealed that she, along with two girlfriends, had seen the monster several months earlier, but her parents hadn't believed them at the time. There had also been a situation involving landowner Bob Scott's goats: 21 in all had mysteriously vanished in recent months, although some of their carcasses had turned up in the nearby woods. During the course of investigation, Larry uttered the humorous name "Hawley Him" and it well and truly stuck.

My own visit to the sleepy little town of Hawley didn't reveal any additional details. One woman who I spoke with at City Hall did remember the incident and admitted that she was still good friends with Renee McFarland, who apparently didn't like to talk about it too much anymore. I visited the property where Bob Scott's ranch had been located. It is currently under new ownership and the area is still very rural, with patches of thick brush surrounding the pastures. The nice lady who I spoke with there was not aware of the Hawley Him. Since there have been no subsequent reports, we can only assume that he has long since moved on to terrorize the populace in new and different haunts. Indeed, perhaps the "Him" relocated south to the community of Hamilton, Texas, which lies in the central part of the state.

In 1992, Bigfoot reports began to surface around Hamilton, when a mysterious Daniel Fisker wrote to the local paper about a sighting he and his family had while driving home from Stephenville one evening. According to Fisker's letter, the family had spotted a giant man-like

Above: The Kelly Bigfoot Location (Ken Gerhard)
Below: The Kelly Bigfoot Manhole Cover (Ken Gerhard)

Above: The lair of the Junction Bigfoot (Ken Gerhard)
Below: Where the San Antonio Sasquatch roams (Ken Gerhard)

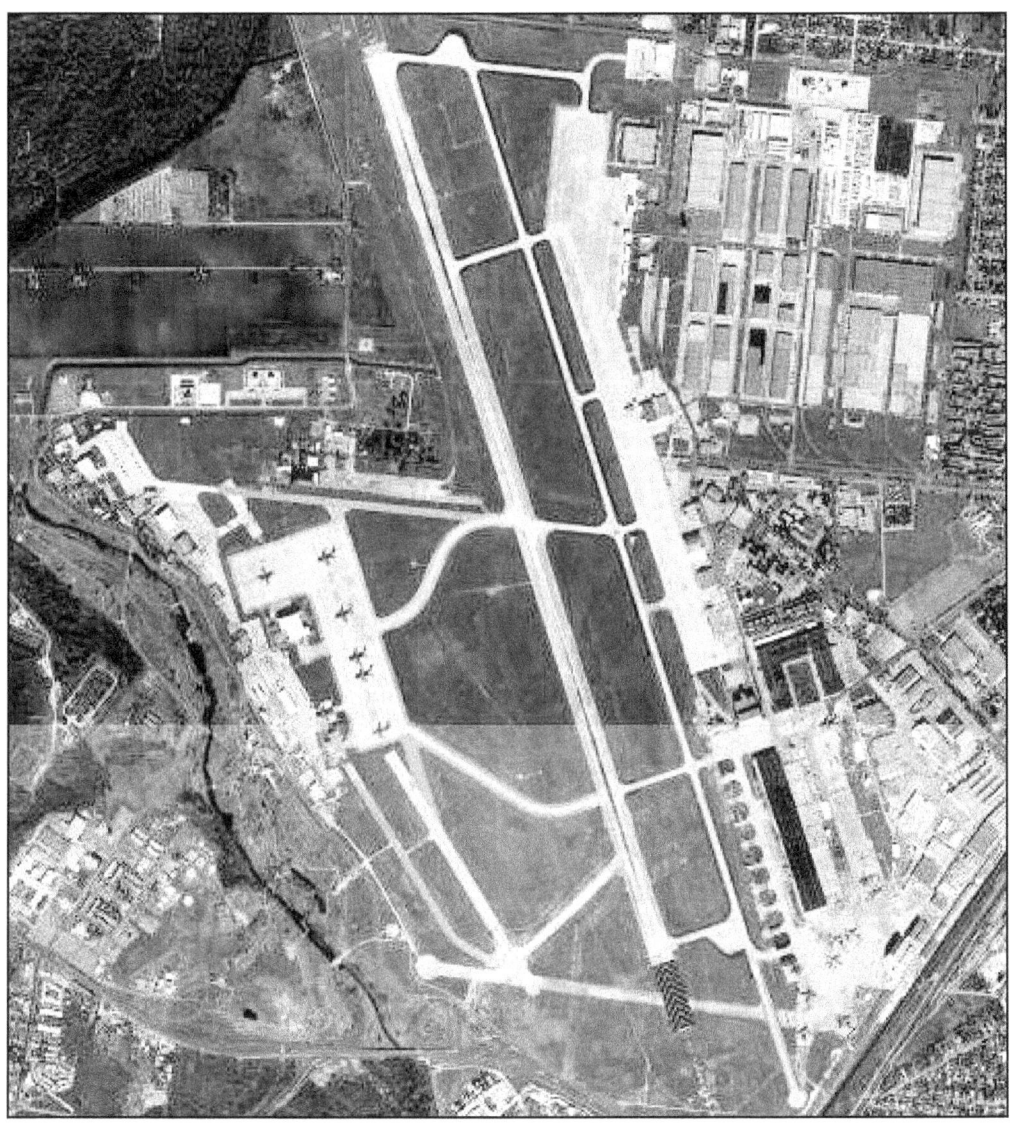

Kelly AFB - A Haunt of Bigfoot (United States Geological Survey)

Above: A Bigfoot Teepee at Ray Roberts Lake (Nick Redfern)
Below: Caddo Lake, home to the East Texas Bigfoot (Nick Redfern)

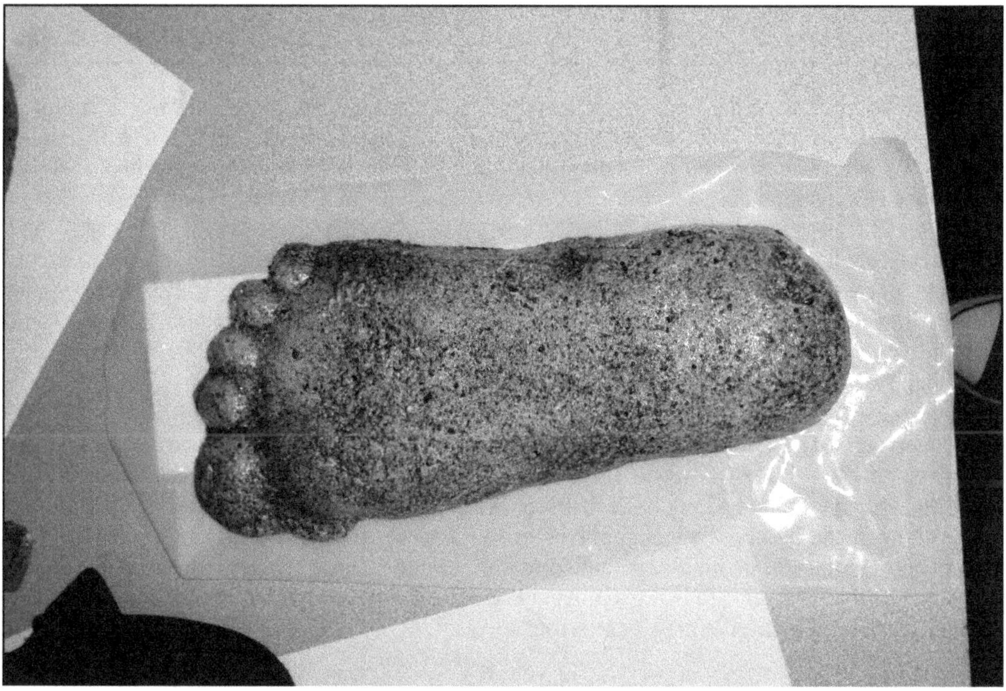

Above: Bigfoot print (Nick Redfern)
Below: Sasquatch lurks at Ray Roberts Lake (Nick Redfern)

creature on the bank of the Leon River. Fisker described the creature as follows: "Standing I would say, approximately seven to eight feet tall, weighing probably between 400 to 500 pounds. Its body was covered with hair. It had long arms that extended down to its knees. Its face looked almost human."

The letter concluded: "It looked at us and growled a low moan, showing four fang-like teeth, two on top, two on bottom, and the rest flat like humans. Then it hurled over the guard rail and ran off into the night toward the brush along the river." Apparently no-one in Hamilton had ever heard of a Daniel Fisker. So, it was assumed that whoever wrote the letter might have been using a pseudonym in order to carefully avoid any potential ridicule.

The letter did, however, prompt other eyewitnesses to come forward, including well-known Hamilton resident Hilda Lunsford. Hilda also wrote the newspaper a letter describing a confrontation she had one morning back in 1985. While driving between Olin and Cranfills Gap, Hilda claimed she observed a giant animal step out into the road, right in front of her car. The thing was standing on its hind-legs, and Hilda, quite understandably terrified, quickly locked her doors and waited for it to make a move. "It looked right at me and it had the face of an ape and it was a big, black something," she wrote.

When the newspaper's editor, Roger Miller, was interviewed by a reporter from the *Dallas Morning News* about the incidents, he confessed that: "We've had numerous telephone calls and people stopping us on the street, some of who really didn't want to reveal their identity. There are people who believe they have seen something."

In the same article, a woman who worked at Hamilton City Hall stated that: "It is out there, and it's been out there for several years."

Bigfoot reports are generally associated with the dense, forested areas of North America. But there have been a smattering of sightings in the desert region that surrounds El Paso, especially near Horizon City to the east. The Horizon City Monster, as it has become famously known, first gained notoriety when an article appeared in the *El Paso City Times* on July 31, 2003.

According to the article, at some point in 2001, retired secretary Cecelia Montanez was driving near Eastlake Boulevard and Darrington Road, when she spotted something leaning over a dead coyote by the side of the pavement. As Cecelia drew within a few hundred feet of it she was shocked when the animal stood upright on two legs like a man, appearing to be more than seven feet tall. Cecelia could see that the being was covered with short bleached burgundy-colored hair. Its body appeared muscular and ape-like and it had a lower jaw that seemed to protrude like that of a bulldog. She also noticed that its ears were pointy. The creature began walking toward the desert, as a man would, and climbed atop a sand dune. Cecelia watched the thing as it jogged down the other side of the dune and vanished from sight, as if possibly descending into a cave.

When her car reached the spot where the monster had been and where the dead coyote was located, Cecelia came to a stop and observed that the head of the animal had been removed and tossed about 15 feet away into the desert. Cecelia was very understandably afraid to leave the safety of her vehicle at the time, but later returned to the scene with her husband and a friend, though by then the coyote carcass was nowhere to be found at all. No caves were found in the area, either.

Cecelia remembered how she had read about a series of Bigfoot sightings by several teenagers at the Horizon City golf course, back in September of 1975. The incidents had been investigated by Deputy Sheriff Bill Rutherford at the time. 14 year old Billy Fuller and 15 year old Kathy Ellis evidently were the first to spot the creature. They flagged Rutherford down as he was cruising by the golf course on a patrol, but by then the thing had vanished. Next, 15 year old Bill York got a good look at the monster on the driving-range and could see that it had a flat face, with sunken eyes, pointy ears and a jutting jaw. Yet another youth claimed that he shot at the beast six times with a rifle at close range, with seemingly no effect whatsoever, and no blood trail left behind either – which is very typical in cases where witnesses have attempted to shoot and kill a Bigfoot. All of the eyewitnesses agreed that the creature stood about eight feet tall.

In October of 2002, a year after her first encounter, Cecilia was driving home on a rainy night when, incredibly, she spotted the monster once again. This time it was standing in her neighbor's driveway and its eyes reflected red like those of a cat when the beams from her headlights hit them. She watched in shock as the animal dropped down on all fours, running swiftly down the street and out of sight.

As word of the strange, hairy visitor spread around Horizon City, other residents began coming forward. An 80 four year old woman remembered how her mother used to warn her to bring in the cattle before dark, or else the "gorillas" would get them. A member of the local Mescalero Indian tribe claimed that he and his wife had seen the monster and that it had stolen some of their chickens. And, in similar fashion, a camper named Brooks told about how she was awakened in the night by a large hairy man-like creature, whose eyes reflected yellow in her campfire light. She watched the thing stare at her for two minutes until it departed, leaving behind it "an odor like a stale pond".

A recent report from west Texas involves a 52 year old truck driver and former law enforcement officer hauling groceries from Junction to San Angelo along U.S. 83 early on the morning of January 1, 2006. As he approached a small bridge, the driver spotted an eight foot tall humanoid with long, rust-colored hair and a human-like face standing by the guardrail, as if waiting for the truck to pass. The driver's family persuaded him to report his sighting to a group of researchers, and subsequently the encounter was included in a Texas lifestyle magazine article about Bigfoot sightings in the Lone Star State.

It seems that man's continuing encroachment may very well, in essence, be driving these remarkable and rare hominids into remote, unpopulated areas like the deserts of the American south-west. If we are to believe that we share our planet with a species of elusive, human-like beasts that inhabit the remote expanses of our wilderness areas, then we must surely include the Lone Star State as part of their vast terrain.

Breaking News!

On Tuesday, December 1, 2009, I received the startling news that there had been a Bigfoot sighting on the west side of San Antonio during the previous night. Since that time, I have been involved in a deep and still on-going investigation of the case, which has received quite a bit of publicity, both locally and on the internet. I've spent considerable time at the location of the encounter, which lies just a mere 12 miles from my home, and I have also been allowed access to the original police report on the matter. Unfortunately, at the time of writing, the eyewitnesses have not been located. But, there is their recorded 911 call, which has now been made public.

Here is what we know so far, at least: Just before midnight on the evening in question, a San Antonio police officer responded to a call from a homeless woman named Jennifer. The woman and her partner claimed that they had witnessed a huge hairy figure walking on two legs, picking up a dead deer and then proceeded to carry it away. The couple, who, apparently, were living in a tent in the woods at the time, also reported that the creature emitted a foul odor and that it made both screeching and howling noises as it retreated towards a nearby water tower, snapping branches as it quickly fled the area.

The responding officer found the witnesses to be completely sober and rational, but quite understandably frightened. He decided not to search for the creature, and indeed, the police have been highly reluctant to have any further involvement in the affair. The somewhat residential location, which lies near the intersection of Loop 1604 and Highway 151 near *Sea World*, is wooded and lies next to a water treatment facility.

Not surprisingly, the pair have since moved out of the area, and as a result of the fact that the weather has gotten cold and wet in the interim, there is speculation that they could be staying in a nearby homeless shelter. In addition, the phone number that is listed on the police report is bad. It rings a department store, thereby frustrating all attempts to track the witnesses down and ultimately raising far more questions than definitive answers.

Local reporter Joe Conger and I determined that the sighting almost certainly took place at a dump site, where a bag full of food (presumably belonging to the couple), along with the remnants of an abandoned campfire, had been left behind. My own searches of the area have revealed no tracks, hair or other evidence and I have not been able to locate any remains of the deer carcass either.

Gulf Coast Bigfoot Research Organization investigator Rick Tullos did discover one foot-like impression that was 13 inches long, and I have found a number of animal bones and empty food containers strewn throughout the area, so a lot of animals are probably drawn to that particular spot. The local news stations have been running broadcasts about the incident and I have now been made aware of other Bigfoot sightings in the area too.

There has also been rampant speculation that the culprit could possibly have been an escaped monkey from the Southwest Research facility (ironically founded by Bigfoot pioneer Tom Slick), based on incidents at a south-side auto body shop where workers spotted an animal resembling a monkey in and around their dumpster. It goes without saying, of course, that Jennifer's description of the beast she saw most assuredly does not resemble a monkey, nor are monkeys known to carry off deer.

On one trip out to the sighting location, I heard some loud, brush-popping noises in the woods, but I wasn't able to accurately pinpoint the source. Less than a week after the report surfaced, the area was plowed over by heavy machinery – which was very strange and convenient timing indeed.

The Big Thicket is a place of mystery (Paraview Books)

Chapter VI
Big Thicket Beasts
(Nick Redfern)

The Big Thicket most assuredly lives up to its name and its strange reputation: it is an 80,000-plus acre area of East Texas's Piney Woods, and is a truly huge and majestic sprawling tangle of rivers, swampland, and incredibly thick forest comprised of cypress trees, short-leaf pines, and gigantic trees of oak and beech, where, local folklore earnestly asserts: "You'll find every critter in there from crickets to elephants."

Well, don't take that too literally; however, the Big Thicket is indeed home to a very wide range of creatures, including armadillos, alligators, panthers, bobcats, and a large array of snakes. And had you been on the scene around 10,000 years ago, you might well have found yourself confronted by bison, camels, tapirs, giant sloth, beavers, saber-toothed tigers, and even marauding packs of wolves. In addition, three groups of Native American Indians made their home in and around the Thicket: the Atakapas, the Caddos, and the Alabama-Coushattas. The Big Thicket is the rumored home of much more too, however, including menacing Bigfoot-type beasts, no less.

Certainly, absolutely no-one knows more about this than Rob Riggs, an acclaimed journalist and author who has delved deeply into the myriad mysteries of the Big Thicket for years, and whose book on this very subject – *In the Big Thicket: On the trail of the Wild Man* – is definitive reading for anyone and everyone fascinated with the cryptozoological mysteries of the Lone Star State.

Before we get to Bigfoot, however, when I met Rob for the first time in early 2003, he told me he had heard intriguing stories concerning sightings of so-called wild men who roamed deep within the Big Thicket. Interestingly, so the stories went, there was a quiet belief and acceptance among some of the local folk of the area that what people were actually seeing were, incredibly, surviving remnants of those aforementioned Native American Indian tribes who were still stealthily making the depths of the Big Thicket their home. That such remnants could still be hiding out in the woods of Texas is notable and thought provoking in the extreme! But, can we entirely rule out such a scenario? Those knowing souls that live on the fringes of the Big Thicket might very well say "no".

Bragg Road – or Ghost Road as everyone in the area calls it – and its immediate surroundings is where the vast majority of all the Bigfoot encounters have occurred. It can be found deep in the heart of the Big Thicket, and commences at a curve on Farm-to-Market Road 787, which is only a brief distance from the town of Saratoga. At the turn of the 20th Century, the Santa Fe Railroad created a survey line from Bragg Road to Saratoga, purchased a right of way, and duly opened up the Big Thicket forest with a railroad. As a result, the Saratoga train started to make daily journeys to the nearby city of Beaumont, carrying people, lumber, livestock and much more. But there's more, too: stories and legends of ghostly, floating balls of light, generally seen after sunset, began to surface in the 1940s, 1950s and 1960s, as more and more folk started to travel the roads of the Big Thicket and built homes for themselves in the surrounding areas.

Earnest attempts to try and rationalize what the lights may be have been put forward for years: there are those who subscribe to the wholly down-to-earth explanation that people are merely seeing, and misinterpreting, car headlights. Others consider the lights of the Big Thicket to be somewhat akin to so-called swamp gas, while some commentators have theorized that the lights are similar to the far more well-known Marfa Lights – which can also be found in the state of Texas.

But, even if the Big Thicket ghost lights have down-to-earth origins, this still does not detract from the fact that there are some seriously strange critters inhabiting this heavily wooded region too. Indeed, take careful note of the following story from Rob Riggs, as told to him by the primary witness, John.

"John's family home is on the edge of the Trinity River swamps near Dayton. One night he heard a disturbance on the porch where he kept a pen of rabbits. He investigated just in time to see a large dark form make off with a rabbit in hand. John impulsively followed in hot pursuit, staying close enough to hear the rabbit squeal continuously, not really knowing what he was chasing or what he would do if he caught it. It was a short distance through thick woods to the bank of the river. Standing on the high bank in the moonlight he watched dumb-struck as what looked like a huge ape-like animal swam to the other side of the river, easily negotiating the strong current, and never letting go of the rabbit."

As Rob also carefully notes: "Like its Bigfoot and Yeti counterparts, the Big Thicket wild man has reportedly left clear tracks on a number of occasions… An expert Big Thicket guide told me of several sets of unusually large barefoot prints he had once come across in the vicinity of Black Creek deep in the Rosier Unit of the Big Thicket Preserve and miles from the nearest

Mysteries of the Big Thicket (Nick Redfern)

GHOST ROAD: THE BIG THICKET LIGHT

GHOST ROAD RUNS ARROW STRAIGHT THROUGH TERRITORY THAT WAS ONCE THICKET, CYPRESS BRAKE, BAYGALLS AND LOBLOLLY PINES. IT BEGAN AS THE BED OF A BRANCH RAIL LINE OF THE GULF, COLORADO AND SANTA FE THAT RAN BETWEEN THE TOWNS OF BRAGG AND SARATOGA TO PROVIDE ACCESS TO THE TIMBERLANDS OF THE AREA. AT THE SOUTHERN END OF THE LINE WAS THE McSHANE LUMBER COMPANY OPERATION AT DEARBORN. TALES OF A GHOSTLY LIGHT BEGAN EVEN AS THE LINE WAS IN SERVICE, BEFORE AUTOMOBILES RAN THROUGH THE AREA.

THE STORIES CONTINUED AFTER THE LINE WAS CONVERTED TO A COUNTY ROAD IN THE 1930s. ARTHUR FULLINGIM, OUTSPOKEN EDITOR OF THE KOUNTZE *NEWS*, PUBLISHED ACCOUNTS OF GHOST LIGHT SIGHTINGS, WHICH BROUGHT WIDESPREAD ATTENTION AND INTEREST. THE ROAD BECAME A POPULAR SITE FOR TRAVELERS, YOUNG COUPLES AND OTHERS INTERESTED IN THE PHENOMENON, KNOWN AS THE GHOST, BRAGG, BIG THICKET OR SARATOGA LIGHT. EXPLANATIONS OVER THE YEARS HAVE INCLUDED THE NATURAL—SWAMP GAS OR REFLECTION OF PHOSPHORIC FOXFIRE; THE HISTORICAL—GOLD HIDDEN BY SPANISH SOLDIERS AND EXPLORERS; AS WELL AS THE SUPERNATURAL—THE SPIRITS OF A RAIL WORKER SEARCHING FOR HIS LOST HEAD, A GROOM LOOKING FOR HIS MURDERED BRIDE, A LOST HUNTER, DISGRUNTLED RAIL WORKERS OR JAYHAWKERS.

IN ADDITION TO ITS PLACE IN POPULAR LORE, THE ROAD'S ONCE DENSE TIMBER STANDS ATTRACTED DEVELOPMENT AND LUMBER INTERESTS. FOR DECADES, COUNTY OFFICIALS DISAGREED WITH OTHERS, INCLUDING NOTED BIG THICKET CONSERVATIONIST R.E. JACKSON, OVER THE ROAD'S IMPORTANCE. IN THE LATE 1990s, IT FINALLY BECAME A PROTECTED RESOURCE. TODAY, IT DRAWS VISITORS ENTICED BY ITS FLORA AND FAUNA, AS WELL AS BY ITS MYTHIC, GHOSTLY LIGHTS.

(2003)

The Big Thicket's Ghost Road (Nick Redfern)

Above: The woods of the Big Thicket. (Nick Redfern)
Below: The Big Thicket's Ghost Road at night (Nick Redfern)

Preparing to investigate the Big Thicket in 2005 (on the left) SMiles Lewis and (on the right) Paul Deveruex (Nick Redfern)

paved road. He had thought they were a bit odd at the time but just assumed that they had been made by an extraordinarily big, old boy. When I pointed out the problem with this assumption, he agreed that it was unlikely that any normal person, big or not, would be walking about barefoot in the Thicket, which has virtually every description of thorn, sticker and spiny vine, not to mention stinging insects and snakes."

Similarly, there is the tale of an elderly man named Dwight, who resides in the relatively nearby Texas town of Nederland, and who personally saw a large and lumbering ape-like creature crossing a road close to the Big Thicket's Bragg Road late at night in the winter of 1978/1979. Dwight described the beast as being around seven feet in height, jet black in color, and with a head that sat squarely on its wide shoulders. He added that the creature moved slowly across the road, and swung its arms as it did so, but did not appear fazed or at all concerned by the fact that the headlights of Dwight's car illuminated its face.

Interestingly, and in a situation that eerily parallels some of the more mysterious cryptozoological encounters on record, when Dwight came within around 50 yards of the creature, both the engine and headlights on his car failed. It was only when the beast had departed into the woods that Dwight was able to re-start his vehicle once again. And, as a result he has, today, become a solid adherent of the theory that the Big Thicket wild man is some form of paranormal or supernatural entity, rather than merely a beast of a conventional, flesh and blood nature.

In the early part of 2005, Rob Riggs planned to hold, in the city of Austin, Texas, a conference on the subject of ghost lights, and the links between that same phenomenon and sacred sites, stone circles, and Bigfoot-like entities. And thus was born the *Texas Ghost Lights Conference* that came to fruition on June 11 of that year at Austin's First Unitarian Universalist Church. Lecturers included Rob Riggs, Jim Bunnell, British ghost light authority Paul Devereux, and me. Jim was the author of two books on the infamous Marfa Lights: *Night Orbs* and *Seeing Marfa Lights*. In addition, he was an aeronautical and mechanical engineer by profession, and had retired in 2000 from BAE Systems as Director of Mission Solutions for various U.S. Air Force programs.

As well as doing all the hard work to ensure that the conference went full steam ahead, Rob also announced the establishment of what he called the *Bragg Road Project*. Basically, it was to be a two-day and two-night excursion to the depths of the Big Thicket that was to commence directly after the *Texas Ghost Lights Conference* was over. So, on Sunday, June 12, all of the speakers, as well as S. Miles Lewis of the Austin-based *Scientific Anomaly Institute*, and two conference attendees named Renee and Nancy, met for breakfast and then made our collective way to our final destination: the heart of those mysterious woods of the Big Thicket.

Bragg Road can most definitely be a strange and unsettling locale even during the day. After darkness has fallen, to describe it as ominous, oppressive and foreboding would be a huge understatement. A careful vigil was kept on the first night, until around 4.00 a.m., during which time – to our astonishment – several ghost lights put in appearances. However, the wild men and the Bigfoot-style entities did not.

On the following day, I had the fortunate opportunity to interview a man named Gerald, who divulged startling details of his own encounter with a monstrous beast within the Big Thicket years earlier, and which was acutely similar to the aforementioned testimony of witness Dwight.

Gerald told me that his sighting took place in the summer of 1977 – and just about as midnight was looming too. The location was right around the area's Old Hardin Cemetery; somewhat appropriately too, it might justifiably be said. Without warning, the engine of his vehicle spluttered and its headlights began to dim – something ominous was most assuredly afoot. As he pulled the vehicle to the safety of the side of the road, and at around 20 yards from him, Gerald told me, he saw what he described as a seven foot tall incredibly thin creature covered in dark hair. It walked like a man, Gerald added, but was "leaning forward and swinging [its] arms."

 The encounter barely lasted mere moments, Gerald explained, and the beast disappeared into the shadowy woods. But, perhaps, most intriguing of all was the next development: only seconds afterwards, a basketball-sized ball of light – a classic ghost light in other words – came floating through the trees at a level above the road of about 50 or 60 feet, and from the same, precise location where the hairy man-beast had entered the trees. The aerial phenomenon maneuvered at a very slow pace, until it was ultimately lost from view amid the dense woods on the opposite side of the road. Notably, after both the creature and the ghost light disappeared,

Gerald's vehicle re-started with absolutely no problems at all. Strange indeed.

While I was deeply engaged in the interviewing of Gerald, back at the Big Thicket dramatic events were unfolding, as Rob Riggs noted in the following email:

"Renee had a frightening experience Monday night. We split up into teams of two and spread out about a mile apart. Renee was paired with Nancy. Nancy walked down the road briefly away from Renee. Renee said she then heard something walking in the woods off the road directly behind her that sounded large. She said whatever it was, was large enough to snap twigs, and she said that it seemed to be moving stealthily, as if it were trying to sneak up on her. She panicked, locked herself into her van and drove off, leaving Nancy to fend for herself. Several hours later she was still shaken and still had goose bumps. Such irrational panic is not characteristic of Renee. She is a ghost hunter and has many times been in creepier situations than being on Bragg Road. She has even gone to cemeteries alone just to test her mettle. There are theories that the creatures deliberately provoke such panic reactions through chemicals in their scent or by mental projection of energy. Renee, Nancy and I also saw a peculiar light. It looked somewhat like a firefly but actually left a solid streak 10 to 15 feet in length that was brilliant bluish-white in color. It happened near a power line, and it was suggested that it might have been some kind of surge on the power line itself. But what could cause such a surge? That, in itself, would be suggestive of an electromagnetic anomaly."

The myriad monstrous mysteries of the Big Thicket would seem destined to continue.

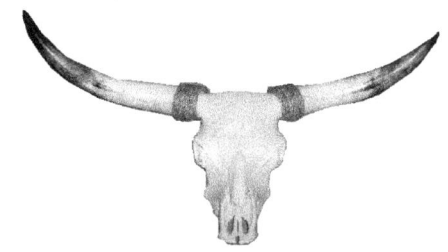

Chapter VII
Monsters of the Dark Waters
(Ken Gerhard)

E ven the most ardent and vociferous of all skeptics will admit that our planet's oceans and waterways remain some of the most unexplored places on planet Earth. Who can truly say what unknown, strange life forms may lurk beneath the great, unseen depths, just waiting to be discovered by enterprising monster hunters of the Gerhard and Redfern kind? For centuries, the sailors and fisherman who traverse those water passages have told memorable and jaw-dropping tales of enormous sea serpents and other mysterious creatures. And, you may not be surprised to learn, the waterways of Texas have spawned many such amazing and eye-opening tales too.

On the afternoon of May 13, 1872, Captain A. Hassel, of the Norwegian ship *St. Olaf*, logged nothing less than a sea serpent sighting off the coast of the Texan city of Galveston. Hassel recorded in his ship's log that: "One of the men sang out that he saw something on the weather bow, like a cask on its end. Presently another one called out that he saw something rising out of the water like a tall man. On a nearer approach we saw it was an immense serpent, with its head out of the water, about 200 ft. from the vessel. He lay still on the surface of the water, lifting his head up, and moving the body in a serpentine manner."

The report continued: "What we could see, from the after part of the head, was about 70 ft. long and of the same thickness all the way, excepting about the head and neck, which were smaller, and the former flat, like the head of a serpent. It had four fins on its back, and the body of a yellow greenish color, with brown spots all over the upper part and underneath white. The whole crew [was] looking at it fully for ten minutes before it moved away."

Moving on, the *Dallas Morning News* newspaper reported on October 26, 1899, the following startling story: "The sea serpent has been seen in the gulf. Captain Gus Christiansen of the tug

Charles Clarke reports that while on the way to Horn Island with a tow of a mud scow, a dredge and another vessel for the work there, he passed within 40 feet of the reptile and was able to get a good view of it. It was apparently about seventy five feet long. Long fins protruded from the surface of the water, which was very calm and resembled a sea of glass. It had flippers on the side with which it propelled itself.

"Publicity brought forth story of a Captain Carrol, who said that 'one day last summer' he saw a 'horrible thing' in the waters of Galveston that was 'the queerest looking thing I ever saw. It had its mouth open and was as big as an apple barrel. It appeared to be all head. From the back of the head was a sort of long horn or tail as big around as that iron post supporting the awning, and the body was covered with green hair.'"

An even more colorful sea serpent account appeared in the *New York Times* on June 30, 1908. According to the *Times*' article, the steamship *Livingstone* of the Texas-Mexican Line was bound from Galveston to Frontera, Mexico at a place called Three Bells, when the sighting occurred. Fifteen eyewitnesses, including Captain G.A. Olsen and four of his crew members, claimed they all observed a gigantic sea serpent off the port bow: "The ship got within sixty feet of the creature and for fifteen minutes stood by while all on board viewed the serpent through glasses."

The article states: "It was apparently sleeping, and was not less than two hundred feet long, of about the diameter of a flour-barrel in the centre of the body, but was not as round. The head was about six feet long by three feet at the widest part. The color was dark brown and near its tail were rings or circles that appeared larger in circumference than the body at that point. As it swam away the tail was erected, and a rattling noise as loud as that made by a Gatling-gun in actions startled the watchers on the Livingstone."

Despite the more whimsical aspects of this report, I can personally attest to the fact that the Gulf of Mexico does conceal some very weird creatures indeed, having once personally hauled in a hideous thing called an oarfish from the Galveston jetties. Oarfish, whose most striking characteristic is a long serpentine body, can obtain lengths up to 36 feet, making them absolute prime candidates to explain some sea serpent reports.

But what are we to make of those reports that stem from Texas's numerous rivers and lakes? There are some vague, old references to sightings of monsters in the Brazos River and also at a place called Klamath Lake. The most oft-mentioned lake monsters in the Lone Star State, however, are the mammoth catfish that have been reported in several Texas reservoirs. These accounts are no doubt related to the urban legends that stem from other bodies of water around the United States, of car-sized catfish that are said to be capable of swallowing a man whole. In a re-occurring theme, the divers who perform maintenance below large dams occasionally encounter these monsters near the bottom.

In truth, catfish, just like sharks, possess a soft skeleton consisting of cartilage and can definitely grow to massive sizes – if they live long enough. They are, in reality, capable of growing throughout the duration of their lives and becoming apex predators. There are gigantic species of catfish found elsewhere around the world too. For example, Europe's Wels catfish (*Silurus glanis*) can grow to be up to eight feet in length and can weigh well over 200 pounds. In the rivers of South America, fisherman regularly catch a species known as the goliath catfish (*Brachyplatystoma*) that can grow to be 12 feet long, and weighing in at over 400 pounds. The endangered Mekong catfish (*Pangasianodon gigas*) of Asia can reach lengths of almost nine feet and can weigh in excess of 600 pounds!

Iconic author Mark Twain once wrote about a 250 pound catfish that was spotted in the Mississippi River, so it is quite conceivable that some truly gigantic specimens may exist somewhere in North America. There are two different species of catfish in Texas that are known to grow quite large. The flathead catfish (*Pylodictis olivaris*) can be found swimming deep in the currents of rivers and lakes and have been known to obtain a maximum weight of 120 pounds. The blue catfish (*Ictalurus furcatus*) can grow just as big, or perhaps even bigger. In 2005, for example, a 121 pound, blue catfish (which was a state record) was caught in Lake Texahoma, which borders the states of Texas and Oklahoma. Given the catchy and appropriate name of Splash, the fish was kept alive and sent to the state fisheries museum at Athens, Texas. Within a few months of his capture, I arranged to visit the museum in order to see Splash in person, so to speak, and was duly impressed by his mighty girth. He actually seemed quite friendly, swimming up to the glass as if to say "hello" to me... or, perhaps, he was wondering how I might taste!

A reference to giant catfish dwelling in Texas's Lake of the Pines appears in Loren Coleman's book *Mysterious America*. I had a chance to spend a couple of days at the lake during 2004 and used the opportunity to speak with some of the locals in order to gather information as to whether or not a giant fish might actually be lurking within its depths. I learned that, according to a very engaging local legend, Lake of the Pines is, in fact, home to an enormous catfish named Oscar that, so the story goes, swam into the slightly ajar window of a sunken Cadillac car when he was but a small hatchling. The legend states that Oscar made a very happy home for himself in the underwater car and voraciously ate anything and everything else that dared to swim through its open window. That is, until he grew so big and fat that he got stuck inside the submerged vehicle. Oscar eventually, and fortunately, made good his escape by smashing his way through the car's windshield! The locals believe that Oscar still inhabits the lake to this very day. And long may he do so.

During the summer of 2005, I joined my friend, well-known outdoorsman and cryptozoologist Chester Moore Jr., on a giant catfish expedition, at Lake B.A. Steenhagen in the far southeastern part of the state. Chester, a respected wildlife writer and fishing expert who grew up in nearby Orange County, had heard stories of monster-sized catfish in Lake B.A. Steenhagen ever since he was a young boy.

An experienced scuba diver, Chester has forayed into shark-infested waters off the coast of California, so he is most certainly no novice. We mutually agreed that he would actually dive the lake's murky depths and scour its deep channels, while I scanned below the surface with underwater cameras. Ultimately, the water proved to be far too murky and clouded with excessive amounts of vegetation, algae and mud. As a result, our visibility was severely impeded and we didn't observe any large fish in the lake that day. Our fish-finding sonar didn't turn up anything significant, either.

Lake Granbury, which lies just west of the city of Fort Worth, is apparently home to a monster with the colorful name of One Eye. According to an internet website, early Spanish settlers used to whisper about a giant serpent that was rumored to inhabit the lake. Rumors of something unusual living in Lake Granbury have apparently continued into very modern times. There is even an unsubstantiated report which tells of a boat being overturned by something big, and which apparently possessed tentacles. This may not be as far-fetched as it sounds. Cryptozoologists Nick Sucik and Todd Jurasek were at one time investigating reports of tentacle-possessing monsters at lakes in Oklahoma. Similarly, an angler at Lake Conway in Arkansas actually hooked a mysterious, freshwater octopus during 2003.

Nick Redfern and I visited Lake Granbury one afternoon in the late summer of 2005, in order to size it up. We both agreed that the lake seemed overly shallow and almost small enough to throw a stone across. Just south of Lake Granbury lies Lake Weatherford, said to be home to a creature described as "a monstrous, man-eating, devil-water-cow." Further information on this distinctly whimsical beast appears to be very scarce, to say the least.

Perhaps some lake monster reports can be attributed to the very large and nasty Alligator Gar (*Atractosteus spatula*): a primitive, ancient reptilian-looking fish that can reach lengths of 12 feet and frequently weighs upwards of 300 pounds. These aggressive and short-tempered beasts can be found in rivers and lakes throughout Texas, and I've personally encountered them many times while on freshwater fishing excursions. Alligator gars, which have been known to attack humans on rare occasions, are noted for their double row of numerous, needle-like teeth and appear quite formidable when they roll upon the surface of the water. It's not hard at all to imagine that someone unfamiliar with these prehistoric-looking fish would describe them as monsters if they were to encounter one for the first time.

A very different type of aquatic beast known as the Carvana, was referenced in an 1852 work by famed French author Alexandre Dumas while he was writing about the adventures of an explorer named Aluna. According to the text, Aluna was traveling through Texas in the 1830s, when one of his horses was devoured by such a creature. Dumas wrote: "This monster lives, so it seems, in Eastern Texas out in those vast marshes that present on the surface the appearance of solid ground, but which are actually nothing more than vast lakes of slime. As for the Carvana, this monster is far more destructive, far more dangerous, than the alligator at its worst. However, none has been seen alive."

Dumas summarized: "When the lagoons dry up, or after the rivers change their channels, dead Carvanas have been found, and are known to resemble giant tortoises with shells 10 or 12 feet long and six feet wide. The head and tail are like those of an alligator. Hiding in the mud much as the ant-lion hides in the sands, he awaits."

Apart from the huge dimensions, the description Dumas gives is very reminiscent of the alligator snapping turtle (*Macrochelys temminckii*). The largest freshwater turtles in the Ameri-

Above: Monstrous catfish dwell within White Rock Lake (Nick Redfern)
Below: White Rock Lake weirdness (Nick Redfern)

In years gone by people believed that monsters roamed the seas and lakes of the globe. Now we know better. Or do we?

cas, these ugly highly bad-natured reptiles are very common in the swampy areas of Eastern Texas and possess sharp beaks that can inflict extremely nasty wounds. Although there is an unsubstantiated story about a whopping 400 pound specimen being caught in Kansas' Neosho River, the official record is actually just over 200 pounds.

One of the organizations I'm affiliated with received a report from an anonymous eyewitness who may have encountered a modern Carvana in Cooke County, Texas, during May of 1987. According to the eyewitness, he was driving to college one morning on Highway 82, between Muenster and Lindsay, near Elm Creek, when he spotted what at first appeared to be a large trash bag lying in the road ahead. As the driver approached, he changed traffic lanes in order to avoid an impact with the object and was utterly amazed when the "garbage bag" raised its head and looked directly at him. It was at that moment that the student recognized it as being an enormous dark-colored turtle, described as being: "Two and a half to three feet high and longer than it was tall." A semi-tractor trailer also had to change lanes to avoid the massive turtle, which was crossing the road and heading south in the direction of the creek. Incredibly, the eyewitness estimated that the creature's head was about the size of a baseball.

If the Carvana monster really existed, then perhaps truly gigantic snapping turtles were indeed lurking within the heart of the east Texas swamps only mere centuries ago. Consequently, some of their descendents might very well still remain there too. In a state as big as Texas, and with all of its attendant coastline, rivers and lakes too, it's not at all beyond the realms of possibility that some slimy, diabolical monstrosity is swimming around out there somewhere, just awaiting some lucky (or, perhaps, unlucky) angler to come along.

From my good friend, colleague and co-author of this very book, Nick Redfern, comes a couple of stories of water-based beasts from Dallas's White Rock Lake. Constructed in 1911 as Dallas's very first reservoir, the lake has nearly ten miles of shoreline, dense trees and a winding path for cyclists, joggers and walkers, and is home to a large variety of animals that includes squirrels, rabbits, skunks, raccoons, possums, bobcats, red foxes, and minks, and no less than 54 varieties of reptiles, among which are rattlesnakes, turtles, a whole variety of lizards, and horned toads. Salamanders and frogs also abound, along with an incredible 217 species of bird, including swans, pelicans, seagulls, loons, and all manner of ducks.

A man named Phil Groff told Nick a fascinating tale of a huge catfish that he saw in White Rock Lake in the summer of 1979. Far too shocked to do much at all, Groff merely stared in awe and astonishment at this true leviathan of the deep and watched it for a few moments before its mighty form sank beneath the waters of the lake, never again to resurface. By his own admission, Groff became somewhat obsessed by the presence of the beast, and for a long time spent nearly every spare moment hoping valiantly to see the massive catfish once again. Sadly, he did not. But there may be more than just giant catfish hiding in White Rock Lake.

In early 2005, Nick drove down to Austin to meet with *In the Big Thicket* author, Rob Riggs and a friend and colleague of his named Mike. The purpose: to discuss some potential television work. As they sat and ate a pleasant Mexican lunch, Mike happened to comment that he had a friend who had heard tales of a juvenile alligator having been clandestinely released into the waters of the lake late one night – possibly when its presumed owner could no longer look after it.

Such a scenario is most certainly not impossible, since this is definitely not the first time that an encounter with an out-of-place alligator has been recorded in Dallas. As prime evidence of this, on August 30, 1891, the *Dallas Morning News* reported the following:

"A monster alligator may be seen at Oak Cliff. The reptile is ten feet in length and possesses a set of teeth that is very suggestive. The monster was caught about ten days ago at Bois d'arc Island in the Trinity. Twenty-five miles from Dallas, by S.D. Mathersoon and John Cranch, who brought it to Oak Cliff in a wagon. The alligator was first discovered in a hole or cave on the island, and after persuading him to thrust his head forth, the two men lassoed him and drew him out. It is pronounced among the largest that have ever been caught in the Trinity."

And, perhaps, similar beasts still continue to exist in the larger bodies of waters that can be found in and around the city of Dallas. Maybe they are even thriving too. After all, it is an absolute fact that more than a few Dallas residents do indeed disappear every year, never to be seen or heard of again…

Chapter VIII

Goat Man Terror

(Nick Redfern)

In the very early hours of one particularly fateful morning in the hot and sticky summer of 1969, six petrified residents of the Texan city of Fort Worth raced for the safety of their local police station and related a controversial and amazing story. John Reichart, his wife, and two other couples were parked at Lake Worth – and, yes, it was indeed at the stroke of midnight – when a truly vile and monstrous-looking creature came storming out of the thick branches of a large nearby tree. Reportedly covered in a coat that seemed to be comprised of both scales and fur, it slammed with a crashing bang onto the hood of the Reichart's car and even tried to grab hold of the not surprisingly terrified Mrs. Reichart, before racing off into the pitch black night and the camouflage of the dense, surrounding trees. The solitary evidence of its dark and foreboding presence was a deep foot and a half long scratch along the side of the Reichart's vehicle.

While this specific event rapidly, and unsurprisingly, generated deep media interest, and was actually taken extremely seriously by the Fort Worth police (as prime evidence of this, no less than four police cars quickly headed out to the scene of the Reichart's encounter), it was most certainly not the first occasion upon which Fort Worth officialdom had become the recipient of ominous accounts of diabolical beasts roaming around Lake Worth.

Indeed, until the Reichart's story hit the newspapers, it was a little known fact that for approximately two months the police had been clandestinely investigating reports of a distinctly weird beast that was said to be spooking the locals on a disturbingly regular basis. While some of the officers concluded that at least some of the sightings might have been the work of local kids, wildly running around in ape costumes, others were not quite so sure that fakery was a dominating factor, and took the Reichart's story firmly to heart.

For example, Patrolman James S. McGee conceded that the report John Reichart filed with the Fort Worth constabulary was treated very seriously, as a result of the fact that: "those people were really scared." Of course, the Dallas-Fort Worth media absolutely loved the story, and did their utmost to promote it just about as much as was humanly possible. Notably, one particular feature that appeared in the pages of the *Fort Worth Star Telegram* was written by acclaimed author Jim Marrs – very well known today for his books on 9/11, the JFK assassination of November 1963, UFOs, and countless other conspiracies and cover-ups.

The headline that leapt out of the *Telegram* was a news editor's absolute dream: *Fishy Man-Goat Terrifies Couples Parked at Lake Worth*. Beyond any shadow of doubt, it was this particular story that made the Goat Man both infamous and even a little feared among the residents of Lake Worth. And it would not be long at all before the monster's ugly form surfaced once again. In fact, it was almost 24 hours to the minute: midnight was looming just around the corner and the creature was reportedly seen racing across a stretch of road close to the Lake Worth Nature Center. Interestingly, the prime witness, one Jack Harris of Fort Worth, stated that when he attempted to take a picture of the monster, the flash on his camera failed to work – an odd phenomenon that is curiously and eerily prevalent in reports and encounters involving mystery animals.

The beast, whatever its ultimate nature and origin, was shortly thereafter seen to charge across the landscape to a nearby bluff, with three dozen hyped-up locals in hot pursuit, and all hysterically baying for the blood of the beast. However, the Goat Man wasn't about to become the victim of some crazed Lake Worth posse. He had an unforeseen ace up his sleeve – allegedly, at least: towering over the crowd at approximately ten yards, the Goat Man hurled a huge tire at the group, which resulted in the throng wildly scattering in all directions. One of those present, a man named Jack Harris, said that: "everybody jumped back into their cars" and hauled ass out of the area. The Goat Man had won the day yet again.

But the story was far from over. Even more accounts surfaced, with some witnesses stating that the creature had dark fur or hair all over its body, while others maintained that its coat was overwhelmingly white in color. Then there were disturbing tales of horrific mutilations of animals in the area: dogs, cats and more – most of which surfaced amid theories that the Goat Man had made a home – or, far more likely, a lair – for himself in a relatively small piece of land, called Greer Island, that is connected to the mainland by a small walkway.

The story was on the verge of spinning wildly out of control, when one Helmuth Naumer, who was an employee of the Fort Worth Museum of Science and History, offered the theory that the Goat Man was probably nothing stranger than a pet bobcat that someone had clandestinely released into Lake Worth Park, and one that presumably took a great deal of pleasure in jumping onto people's cars at midnight. Precisely how the bobcat was able to change its color from brown to white, or throw a large tire through the air – for what was estimated to be a distance of no less than 500 feet – remained sadly unanswered however.

Of course, it's not impossible, or unreasonable to suggest, that Naumer's theories might indeed have provided answers to the questions that pertained to at least some of the sightings.

Above: Goat-Man Central (Nick Redfern)
Below: Lake Worth - the domain of the Goat Man (Nick Redfern)

Above: Goat Man Bridge at Denton. (Nick Redfern)
Below: A curious Teepee structure found at the site of the
Lake Worth Goat-Man (Nick Redfern)

However, those same theories most assuredly could not explain the truly surreal photo taken by a man named Allen Plaster, who was a local dress shop owner. Plaster's picture displayed a giant, white-hued beast with a torso that appeared to be constructed out of dozens of cotton balls, and atop which sat a truly tiny head. And while stories and friend-of-a-friend-type tales suggested Fort Worth police had found evidence that some of the sightings were indeed the work of costumed hoaxers, this was an issue that to this day remains very murky and far from being fully resolved.

There is, however, a sequel to the odd affair of the Lake Worth Goat Man. On Saturday, October 3, 2009 – which marked the 40th anniversary of the Goat Man sightings – the first ever *Lake Worth Monster Bash* was held at the lake, and right in the heart of where the monster was originally seen. Or, as it's known today: the Fort Worth Nature Center and Refuge. Well, living only about 20 or 30 minutes away meant I just had to attend. And I'm very glad that I did, as a fine time was had by one and all – even my wife, Dana, whose interest in cryptozoology is (to put it diplomatically!) minimal, had a great time!

I have to confess that when Dana and I set off for the lake around 9.00 a.m. on the morning in question, I did wonder if anyone would actually show up. After all, how many people would want to learn about a 40 year old story of a beast described as being half-man and half-goat in nature? Actually, the answer is: quite a lot! Indeed, by around 11.00 a.m., the car park was practically full, and the crowds were out in full force.

And there was much to do and see too. Recognizing that the Goat Man was (and still is) an integral part of Lake Worth's history, the FWNCR put on a great event. Craig Woolheater and the Texas Bigfoot Research Conservancy were there, highlighting the work of the group. And Sean Whitley, writer, director and co-producer of *Southern Fried Bigfoot* – an excellent documentary on Bigfoot in the American South – had a table promoting his film.

For those who wanted to get firmly into the spirit of the Goat Man legend, there was the *Throw like the Pro – Tire Hurling Contest*, where people could try and recreate the Goat Man's legendary tire-throwing caper of 1969. There was also a hike to Greer Island – that small body of land on the lake where the beast was supposedly seen, as well as a trip to the quarry where the tire-throwing incident occurred. For the children, there was a reading of the book *Cam the Man Hunts for the Spooky Goat Man*, written by local author Stephanie Erb, and a chance for the kids to build their own monster at the *Kids' Monster Headquarters*. In addition, there were some very welcome stalls and displays that highlighted local wildlife, including exotic insects and much more. And there was a musical performance too, from *The Skip Pullig Band*, who performed their new song, titled (what else?): *The Goat Man.*

And it didn't end there: Sallie Ann Clarke, one of the original researchers of the affair and the author of the 1969 book, *The Lake Worth Monster*, had loaned her collection of Goat Man memorabilia to Lake Worth's Hardwicke Visitor's Center, which has a whole section devoted to his Royal Goatness, and which is most definitely well worth seeing. Plus, canoe tours around Greer Island, a chance to feed the island's resident population of huge Bison, and hay rides around the lake were all part of the day's events.

In other words, this was very much a fun, family-oriented, interactive experience that paid homage to the original legend of the Goat Man, but one that also allowed people to learn about the important work of the FWNCR. And it got the kids away from the computers and the TVs for a while, and let them see that there is a real world outside, full of fresh air, mysteries, adventures and much more. All in all, it was a cool, informative and very entertaining day. Here's looking forward to the next Goat Man gig!

Lake Worth is not the only location within the Lone Star State that is associated with the dark and disturbing activities of Goat Man-style beasts. Another such creature of distinctly Goat Man proportions has been regularly reported at the 1884-built Old Alton Bridge in the town of Denton, which is situated approximately an hour's drive outside of the city of Dallas. One legend says that, many years ago, wannabe devil worshippers in the area inadvertently opened up a portal to some hellish realm that allowed the vile beast open access to our world. And now, today, and as a direct result of this reckless action, the Goat Man has no intention at all of returning to the twilight zone from which he originally appeared, hence his deep desire to forever haunt the old steel and wood bridge at Denton.

An even weirder story maintains that the Denton Goat Man's origins can be traced back to a resident of the town who, decades ago, slaughtered his entire family, and was quickly hanged as a punishment for his terrible crime. As the local legend tells it, at the moment he was hung, the man's head was violently torn from his body by the weight of his blubbery form, and for months afterwards his spectral body returned to the world of the living with only one goal in mind: to find itself a brand new head – which it supposedly did by wrenching off the head of an innocent goat that had the great misfortune to be in the area at the time. And so, the Goat Man of Denton was born. Was this merely a tall tale? Of course it was! But that does not take away the fact that local folk, on many occasions, have reported seeing the nightmarish, hoofed one roaming around the woods behind the bridge. In other words, whatever the real origins of Denton's Goat Man, there does appear to be a significant amount of substance to what many merely perceive as an entertaining piece of local hokum and folklore.

Interestingly, only a very short drive from the town of Denton is a very large body of water called Ray Roberts Lake – which, just like its near-neighbor Denton, has played home to monstrous activity for years. In times past, the area was the domain of the haunt of several Native American Indian people, such as the Comanche, the Kiowa and the Tonkawa. And, back in May 1990, it became the domain of an apparently very large predatory beast. Hairy and man-like, its wild screams echoed around the lake after nightfall, leaving those unfortunate enough to hear the eerie sounds in no doubt that something evil and unknown had made Ray Roberts Lake its home.

Interestingly, when I paid a visit to the location in early 2008 with a colleague, Lance Oliver – who runs the Denton Area Paranormal Society – we found in the direct location where the beast was both seen and heard 18 years earlier, a number of curious structures that, within the world of cryptozoology, have become known as "Bigfoot Teepees." These admittedly weird formations are basically comprised of large branches that, more often than not, appear to have been literally torn off the surrounding trees by something possessed of immense strength, and carefully positioned into pyramid-type patterns. Perhaps they are designed as territorial markers and boundaries, or maybe they are meant to attract others of the kind that constructed the formations in the first place.

Most fascinating of all, when Ken Gerhard and I visited Lake Worth in 2005, we found one such teepee deep within the trees that dominate Greer Island – the home of that particular lake's Goat Man. Was this, therefore, the same beast, but on the move? Or are we looking at more than one such unholy entity? Time, we most assuredly hope, will eventually tell. And yet another Goat Man can be found in Texas too: it makes its home on the green, pleasant and tree-covered shores of Dallas's picturesque and tranquil White Rock Lake – which, as we have already learned, may very well be home to a giant catfish and at least one out-of-place alligator.

So the legend goes, on a number of occasions in the late 1970s and the early 1980s, a very weird beast indeed was seen lurking in the shadows of the many trees that dominate White Rock Lake. The encounters usually occurred right as the sun was setting, and daylight was just upon the verge of yielding to the overwhelming blackness that always comes with nightfall. Those who caught sight of the critter described it as somewhat human-like, but much taller than the average man, with a pair of goat-like horns atop its head and a pair of cloven-hoofs instead of feet. This was not your everyday citizen of Dallas, as if I really need to stress such a fact. In fact, the closest thing that the beast seemed to resemble was the legendary Satyrs of ancient folklore and mythology, and the god, Pan.

 The denizen of forests, fields, flocks of animals and shepherds, Pan's domain was the grotto. His range included mountains and valleys, and he had an abiding love of music. He was also greatly feared by all who knew of his sinister existence, chiefly because, in centuries past, Pan had the worrying ability to deliberately induce states of extreme terror in those who crossed his path – hence the now familiar term "Panic attack".

One of the most fascinating accounts pertaining to the Goat Man of White Rock Lake came from a woman named Sandy Grace, who told me she had seen the horny one himself in the summer of 2001. Attempting to burn off a large amount of excess blubber that had developed over the years from an addiction to large cheese-laden Mexican meals, Grace was jogging breathlessly around the lake on the day at issue, when suddenly the Goat Man appeared out of the trees and bounded towards her.

The man-beast, Grace explained, was "big" and his whole body was covered in a slight coarse hair. And, of course, he had the obligatory two horns on his head of a type that no self-respecting Goat Man can ever be seen without. The Goat Man was not intent on sticking around for long however. After apparently generating a deep and overwhelming sense of panic in Grace, he got down on all-fours and disappeared in a flash of light that reminded the witness of a bright camera flash.

Quite clearly, whatever the real nature of the Goat Man, he seems to find himself quite at home in the heart of Texas. And, I say, long may he continue to do so too.

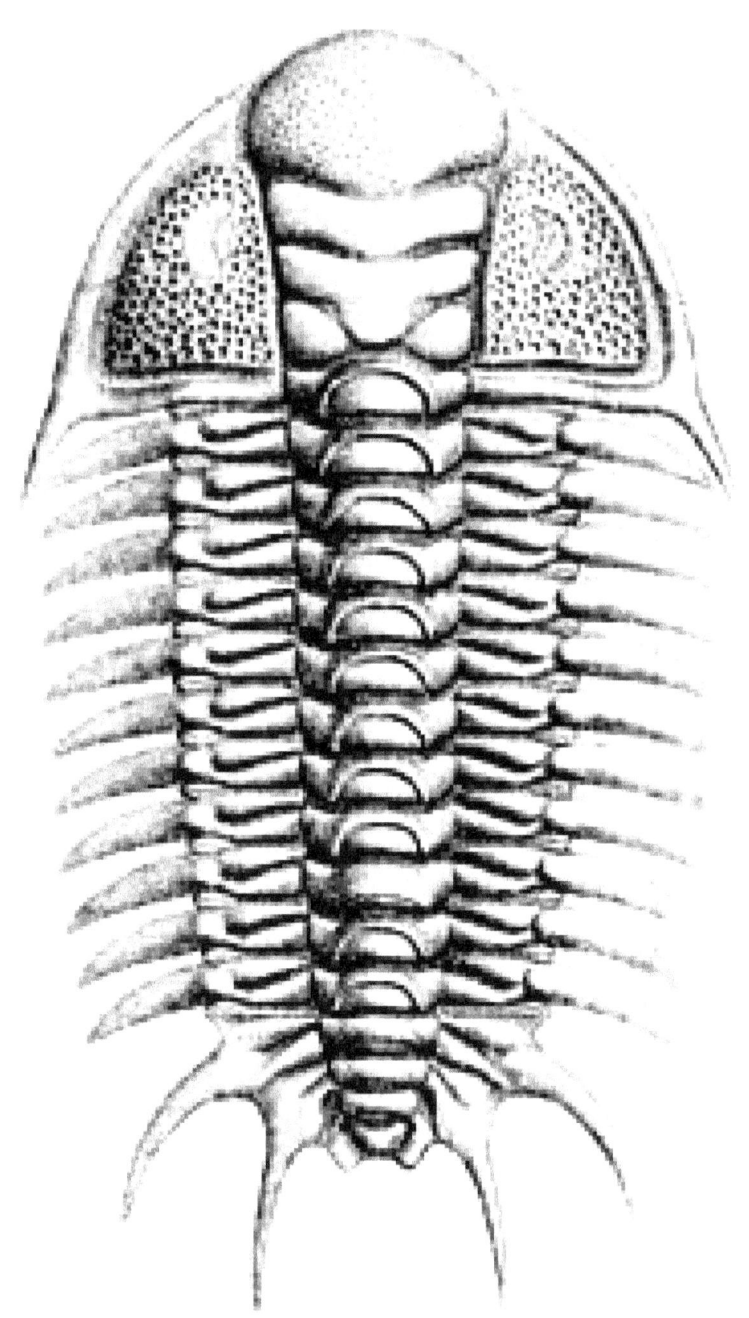

Trilobites were marine arthropods that supposedly became extinct some 250 million years ago. Could a species have survived to 21st Century Texas?

Chapter IX

Fringe Creatures
(Ken Gerhard)

Beyond any shadow of a doubt, the most challenging aspect of being a cryptozoologist is that which deals with reports of strange creatures that do not fit neatly into the context of zoology. It's one thing to embrace the possibility that we share our world with a race of ancient hairy man-giants, or even some surviving leviathan dwelling deep in the heart of a dark Scottish loch. It's quite another, however, to accept the notion that people are describing run-ins with werewolves, gargoyles, goat men and a host of other inexplicable figures from the realms of folklore and mythology. Indeed, it would be quite easy to write off these accounts as the product of overactive imaginations or perhaps even downright fabrications, were it not for the emotional trauma that is directly borne out of these kinds of encounters, and which we have experienced firsthand while conducting investigations into matters of this particular and peculiar nature.

In a state that is as big as Texas, it's not surprising at all that there exist truly mind-boggling reports of creatures that defy our understanding of the natural world, and which are seemingly biological impossibilities. For example, I heard a secondhand account from a friend named Shawn Botella, whose Czechoslovakian-born father worked on the foundations of buildings in Seguin, Texas for many years. Shawn told me about how his father, along with a group of co-workers, was digging deep under an old structure one time when he unearthed an animal that resembled a large trilobite. These are, of course, primitive, fossil arthropods that according to scientists died out around 250 million years ago! As luck would have it, the crab-like, `trilobite` quickly scurried back into the dark crevice from whence it first emerged. Had it not done so, however, today we might very well have in our hands some pretty convincing evidence suggesting that extinction might not be as it has always been portrayed. Exemplifying this premise is the Coelacanth (*Latimeria*), a fish that was presumed to have become extinct millions of years ago; that is, until a living specimen was caught off the coast of South Africa in 1938. Perhaps more living fossils still await discovery, and just maybe some of them can be found in the Lone Star State too.

As I have noted, residents of south Texas have, for decades, been describing close encounters with winged monsters that look like the prehistoric reptiles known as pterosaurs. In a similar vein, the legendary Mountain Boomers of west Texas's Big Bend National Park are purported to be gigantic, bipedal lizards that greatly resemble certain types of dinosaurs. Their name is, apparently, a reference to the thunderous sounds these monstrous reptiles make when they bellow out from the distant canyons. Many old-timers from the foothills claim to know some-one who has stumbled upon these menacing creatures feasting on road-kill, although the original source of these stories is often difficult to pinpoint.

The general description includes a height of about five or six feet, a greenish-brown or dusty color, and most importantly, small forelimbs that resemble arms hence the Boomer's upright posture. This profile definitely matches that of several species of dinosaur, and the region has indeed proven to be fossil-rich, with many notable discoveries being excavated throughout the state. The well-preserved Paluxy dinosaur tracks, located near Glen Rose, stand as curious reminders that the Lone Star State was once inhabited by a myriad of gigantic reptiles, way back in the distant past. But, 64 million years is a very long time for something large and car-nivorous to remain undetected, even in the barren confines of Texas's western deserts.

While investigating reports of these elusive beasts in 1993, researcher Jimmy Ward wrote about running into a family from Connecticut, who claimed to have sighted a Mountain Boomer as they were driving through Texas on their way to California. The family told Ward that the creature looked like something straight out of the movie *Jurassic Park* and that it was enormous. Ward noticed that the father still seemed visibly shaken by his encounter. There is a similar story from Big Bend that involves a car which was nearly run off the road by a "dinosaur" back in the 1970s.

Perhaps not coincidentally, the eastern collared lizard, which is native to parts of the United States, is commonly known as the mountain boomer, and is primarily found within the state of Oklahoma. Oddly, these lizards do possess the ability to run upright on their hind legs when threatened, but they only grow to be about 14 inches in length. Perhaps some Texas Boomer reports might be explained by sightings of collared lizards in their upright posture or maybe even Gila monsters, which are very large and potentially hazardous lizards native to Big Bend. Or, perchance, there really is a lost world, hidden amidst the remote canyons of west Texas. The area is certainly steeped in deep mystery, with the famous, and presently unexplained, Marfa Lights being sighted on a regular basis in the nearby night skies.

If the notion of bipedal lizards seems quite unbelievable, then the suggestion of a humanoid reptile must truly boggle the mind. Yet, occasionally we do hear accounts of so-called lizard men not unlike Hollywood's famous *Creature from the Black Lagoon*, slinking along near the waterways of the Americas. The most famous of these made news all around the country when it apparently attacked a teenager's car in South Carolina during 1988. And Texas may have its own version of the Lizard Man.

Quite recently, for example, I received a report from a motorist who works in Maynard, Montgomery County. While driving to work early one morning near a wooded area the witness claims to have spotted what was described as: "A tall, dark, upright creature… It was at least seven feet tall. It had what appeared to be smooth, shiny, very dark skin. It had no visible body hair. Its arms were very long with long fingers. As the creature ran across the paved road in front of me, it turned its head toward me and I could see that it had large, red eyes."

Further details revealed that the being most definitely had a reptilian appearance, with a greenish color, a large head and a long neck. The witness emphasized the fact that: "It did not run slumped over, but was fully erect."

Then there is the unlikely case of the flying snake seen over Bonham, Texas. According to a newspaper article that was published in the *Bonham Enterprise* back in June of 1873, farmers in the area looked up from their work and were astonished at what they saw. The article stated that: "There appeared to be an enormous flying snake, as large and as long a telegraph pole. It was of a yellow striped color, and seemed to float along without any effort. They (the eyewitnesses) could see it coil itself up, turn over, and thrust forward its huge head as if striking at something, displaying the maneuvers of a genuine snake. The cloud and serpent moved in an easterly direction, and were seen by persons a few miles this side of Honey Grove."

Coincidentally, there are accounts from other 19th century newspapers that describe other sightings of flying snakes – over both Kansas and South Carolina.

One of the most bizarre of all strange beings that haunts the lore of Texas is known as the Houston Batman. The quintessential encounter, as reported within the pages of the *Houston Chronicle*, took place during the early morning hours of June 18, 1953. As a result of the fact that it was a hot and restless night, 23 year old housewife Hilda Walker, and neighbors, 14 year old Judy Meyer and 33 year old tool plant inspector Howard Phillips were sitting on the porch of Hilda's home, located at 118 East Third Street.

Hilda stated: "Suddenly about 25 feet away I saw a huge shadow across the lawn. I thought at first it was the magnified reflection of a big moth caught in the nearby street light. Then the shadow seemed to bounce upward into a pecan tree. We all looked up. That's when we saw it."

Hilda went on to describe the nature of the entity to the newspaper: "It was the figure of a man with wings like a bat. He was dressed in gray or black tight-fitting clothes. He stood there for about 30 seconds swaying on the branch of the old pecan tree… It had the exact appearance of a man dressed in a tight fitting uniform similar to a paratrooper. He was encased in a halo of light."

The trio all agreed that the being stood about six and a half feet tall and said that the strange glow engulfing him was yellow in color. The "Batman" vanished when the light slowly faded out, and right about the time Judy screamed out.

Mrs. Walker also recalled the following: "Immediately afterwards, we heard a loud swoosh over the house tops across the street. It was like the white flash of a torpedo-shaped object… I've heard so much about flying saucer stories and I thought all those people telling the stories were crazy, but now I don't know what to believe. I may be nuts, but I saw it, whatever it was… I sat there stupefied. I was amazed."

Judy added: "I saw it and nobody can say I didn't."

Howard was candid in stating: "I can hardly believe it. But I saw it… we looked across the street and saw a flash of light rise from another tree and take off like a jet." For her part, Hilda dutifully reported the incident to local police the following morning.

As I was once a long-time resident of Houston, I've made attempts to locate the address on East Third Street where the event took place and have found that, today it is no longer in existence, seemingly having been overtaken by the expansion of the nearby Interstate 10. Strangely, the location has seemingly vanished into the void. Some years after I first heard of the Batman, a close friend told me about some fellow employees at Houston's Bellaire Theater, who claimed to have seen a gigantic helmeted man, crouched down and attempting to hide on the roof of a downtown building one night during the 1990s. Perhaps we should seriously consider the possibility that the Houston Batman has returned to haunt his old stomping grounds.

Stories about winged humanoids are not at all uncommon in Texas. During November of 1975, for example, rumors of a four foot tall man-bird, exhibiting both human and avian characteristics, were circulating in Rio Grande City on the Mexican border. The creature was supposedly seen stalking the roof of the town's court house late at night. Tales of a birdman can also be found in Robstown, which is situated near Corpus Christi, and as I discovered while participating in an episode of the television series *Monster Quest*, legends of winged humanoids have a long-standing tradition in northern Mexico, and very close to the border of Texas.

In the mountains surrounding Monterrey, for example, there exist accounts of both tall, feathered man-birds and also flying brujas or witches. In fact, a young Monterrey police officer named Leonardo Samaniego made headlines just about everywhere in January of 2004, when he claimed that his patrol car was attacked by a flying witch adorned in nothing less than a black hooded robe. According to the officer, the entity floated out of a tree and seemed to hover in the air. She then flew at Leonardo's patrol car, viciously clawing at him through the windshield. He quickly threw his car into reverse and called for back-up. Samaniego described his attacker as a hideous, black-skinned hag, who sported a pair of large, black, lidless eyes and claw-like hands. Leonardo was discovered in a state of absolute shock by another officer, just minutes after the encounter. For the next week, Leonardo underwent various tests at the local hospital that confirmed he had been completely sober and of utterly sound mind at the time of the incident.

Above: Lookout Hill - Home of the Ottine Swamp Monster (Ken Gerhard)
Below: Monsters are so much a part of the Texas mythos that they are still sold to holiday-makers today (CFZ)

The macabre folk beliefs of Mexico have influenced the folklore of Texas, and may be behind some of its monsters (CFZ)

Interestingly, and possibly of deep significance to the above story, is the fact that a well-known legend in Mexico and south Texas tells of the Lechuza: a shape-shifting witch who is capable of transforming herself into a large white owl that spends its time crossing the night skies in search of prey. Sometimes a Lechuza will perch in dark tree tops and whistle at her unsuspecting victims who are warned never, ever, to answer back.

The traditional and superstitious people of south Texas have many colorful legends about mysterious phantoms and creatures. La Llorona is a weeping female spirit, so the story goes, who befell a great tragedy in her mortal life. Some say she drowned her two children in a river to appease a lover and then killed herself out of guilt. As a result of her actions, she eternally haunts the rivers and creeks at night, crying out in complete and utter despair. Children are warned to stay away from the water's edge at night, or else La Llorona will drown them. Some residents have even claimed to have had sightings of a ghostly, white female apparition by the San Antonio River after dark.

Similarly, there is a place named Woman Hollering Creek on the city's eastern edge that some believe is supposedly one of her haunts. One version of the story states that La Llorona was horribly disfigured in a fire she had set in an attempt to murder her children. The result of her terrible injuries was that her face came to resemble that of a donkey.

Here however, the legends gets blurred somewhat, because there is also a prominent story in and around San Antonio, which tells of the Donkey Lady. There is, in fact, an old bridge on Applewhite Drive on the city's south side where the Donkey Lady is said to dwell, lurking in the surrounding forests. Some descriptions indicate that she is anthropomorphic, possessing the body of a woman, but with the head and hooves of a donkey. Others say that like La Llorona, she was once a mortal who became disfigured in a fire. Either way, the Donkey Lady was cast out to live deep in the woods. Many people have claimed that they've heard the beating of hooves near the bridge at night, after calling out her name three times. Residents around San Antonio even remember that there was once a well-known phone number, which one could dial in order to hear the sound of the Donkey Lady's hoof-beats drawing ever nearer!

One of my favorite San Antonio-based sagas involves a very dubious character, referred to locally as the Dancing Devil. According to many eyewitnesses, as well as newspaper articles from the time, a dashing, handsome, young man dressed in white entered the *El Camaroncito* night-club on Old Highway 90 one night, around Halloween of 1975. According to all of those who were present, the man was a fabulous dancer and wooed many of the ladies who were in attendance that evening.

As the night progressed, however, things took a very horrific turn when one of the man's dancing partners happened to glance down at his feet. The woman screamed out in terror, broke free of the man's grip and immediately began pointing downward. It was then, amidst a flurry of gasps and shrieks that the patrons noticed the man's shoes had transformed into clawed chicken's feet!

In some versions of the story, his feet had become goat's hooves (perhaps the diabolical offspring of some unholy alliance between the Donkey Lady and Lake Worth's Goat Man?). Either way, it was certainly a bad sign to be sure, as the attendees were now quite sure they were in the presence of none other than the Devil himself. After an uncomfortable silence, the man dashed, or perhaps waddled or galloped, towards the men's room, where he vanished out of an open window. In his wake remained a cloud of smoke, which was accompanied by a strong, sulfuric smell – surely a classic calling card of the horned and forked-tailed dweller of the underworld.

South San Antonio business owner Benjamin Aum told me about another weird episode from the 1970s that he remembered being reported in local newspapers, as well as on some television news broadcasts too. It apparently involved a gargoyle-like monster that most resembled a winged dog. According to Aum, the event had occurred off of Poteet Highway during late 1975 or early 1976. The creature had evidently scratched at the windows of a house and then flown onto its rooftop. That's when the cops were called out – not surprisingly. A number of officers started to shoot at the thing and it quickly disappeared into a wooded area, never to be seen again.

Texas's official state goblin is known as El Cucuy, which is usually, depicted as a tiny, child-like humanoid with large, glowing, red eyes. These shadowy figures are believed to lurk under children's beds or in their closets. Is this simply a legend, or could there actually be a real creature behind the stories of El Cucuy? A few years ago, a resident from San Benito told researcher Guadalupe Cantu that he had spotted a bizarre, little humanoid crawling out of a garbage dumpster. The man had described the being as small and man-like, but covered in hair. He referred to it as "a little vato," and didn't stick around to find out why on earth it had been dumpster-diving.

During January of 2006, a winged version of El Cucuy was encountered by a Texas woman. The incident took place four and a half miles north of a panhandle town called Dickens, which lies east of Lubbock. The young student was driving south on Highway 70 at a place known as Turkey Crossing when she saw the thing. The distraught woman's mother felt compelled to send a letter to an associate of Texas Bigfoot researcher Craig Woolheater.

In the letter she stated: "She [the daughter] noticed that there was something sitting on a wide gate post. She did not know what it was so she slowed down to look. As she got closer, she saw a flesh-colored animal, about three feet tall, crouched on top of the post. It had a round head like an owl and a round, sloped face with a tiny round nose, like a short snout and a slit for a mouth. It had eyes that looked like they were slanted down."

The description continued: "The creature was sitting with its feet together and its knees out, in a bow-legged squat. It had feet like a bird with a set of toes or talons in the back and another set in the front. It had short arms with a flap of triangular skin on the backsides. There was something pointed at the tips of the skin flaps that looked like a bat thumb or claw. It looked like it had paws with four digits on each one and the arms were partially hidden underneath a flap of skin on each side. The skin or short fur was a tan or peach color and it was wrinkled in places like a baby bat."

As the eyewitness attempted to pass, the hideous goblin lurched off of its perch and landed on the road, causing her to swerve. The little monstrosity crouched for a moment and then started to run on two legs while the terrified girl sped off, apparently in tears as she drove home.

My co-author, Nick, was told a very strange story in late 2001 that concerned the sighting of a number of winged, gargoyle-like entities in the town of Littlefield, not at all far from the city of Lubbock, way back in 1946. In other words, the above account is not the only one suggesting strange winged monsters are lurking in and around the Lubbock area.

According to the story told to Nick, the initial event took place around February or March of 1946 – at a large and sinister-looking old house owned by two elderly and eccentric sisters, that could be found on the fringes of the town – albeit no more; since it was reportedly knocked down at some point during the 1970s after having fallen into overwhelming disrepair.

So the legend went, on one particular occasion after sunset, some of the neighborhood kids were playing in the vicinity, and entertaining and thrilling themselves by stealthily wandering around the mysterious property, hoping to catch a glimpse of the two aged and wrinkled hags that lived there. The children got far more than they bargained for, however: as they passed the outside entrance to the old cellar, out crept nothing less than a pair of eight foot tall bat-winged entities, gray in hue, and possessing bright red, glowing eyes.

For a moment or two the kids were rooted to the spot by overwhelming fear and could only watch helplessly as the beasts "hopped around" for a few seconds, before opening their mighty wings and taking to the dark skies; actually, not unlike the villainous star of the two *Jeepers Creepers* movies. At this point, sheer and overwhelming panic set in and the kids raced for home – never again daring to go anywhere near the old house. Whether it was a true story, or merely an old tale cunningly designed to scare the kids of Littlefield into not straying where they weren't wanted, it is one that is still occasionally told in hushed tones among the people of this quiet and isolated west Texas town.

There is a popular rest stop named Buccees that lies along Interstate 10 near Luling, Texas. On one particular occasion, while stopping off there, in order to relieve myself and perhaps purchase some jerky, I noticed that another customer was wearing a t-shirt bearing the legend "*Ottine Swamp Monster*". Below the text was an image of a shaggy man-like hulk lurking among some swampy reeds. Curious to know precisely what kind of t-shirt-worthy monster was stalking the nearby bogs, I made a small diversion.

Ottine Swamp is located just south of Luling on the San Marcos River. It is a brushy thicket, largely surrounded by scenic Palmetto State Park. The area's oldest legends make reference to both indigenous peoples, as well as early Spanish explorers, who would often end up missing if they ventured too deep into the marsh. Some may have fallen victim to the deep mud boils that are capable of swallowing a man whole, or perhaps they ran across something more sinister... something known locally as simply "The Thing."

Longtime resident Berthold Jackson has logged the stories for decades, after running across something one fateful night that he still can't explain. The experience shook him to his foundations. On that occasion, Jackson and his friend Johnny Boehm, of Gonzales, were hunting for rabbits in the swamp one evening about 50 yards apart, when they heard something very large move between them, snapping the brush. But, when the two men shone their flashlights on the spot, expecting to see the source of all the commotion, they were both mystified. There was absolutely nothing there, although they could certainly both hear it moving around.

Jackson knows of other outdoorsmen who have been spooked in the swamp at night. Three fishermen running a trotline, for example, were pursued through the weeds by some unseen force that could be heard but not seen. Similarly, two young hunters and their dogs had been tracking something at the base of Lookout Hill, when suddenly it reared up behind them, causing them to flee in terror. All they could tell for certain was that the thing was huge in size and gray in color.

On another occasion, a couple that was parked at Lookout Hill claimed that something violently shook their car, very nearly pushing it off a cliff. When the driver ran around to confront his attacker, there was no-one there. The stories go on and on. Jackson's son even interviewed a resident who swore that something enormous had shook his mobile home near the swamp on a few occasions, as well as ripping items off of his clothes line. For his part, Berthold has heard weird cries that he cannot explain, and that are somewhere between those of a human and those of an animal. One time, he even found some unusual tracks that curiously resembled a woman's handprint, but with only a mere stub where the thumb should normally be found.

When I arrived at Palmetto State Park, I spoke with one of the rangers on duty. She assured me that she had heard many stories about the Swamp Monster and said that there were indeed those who really believed in its existence. But, she added that no recent reports had been logged; at least as far as she knew. I purchased a nifty, swamp monster t-shirt from the gift shop and got directions to Lookout Hill. When I got to the top, I stared down from the craggy peaks to the dense forest below with a deep sense of awe and wonder. Maybe, I thought, there really is a sinister monster lurking in the Ottine Swamp.

Tales of so-called Swamp Boogers are not uncommon in the bottomlands of the south-eastern United States; phantom bogey-men that terrorize young couples parked in desolate lover's lanes. Much like the bogey-man of old, parents warn their children to stay inside when the sun goes down or else the Boogers will get them. These monsters have frequently been linked to Bigfoot activity due to their huge and hairy appearance, as well as their generally unpleasant odor and demeanor. But, in the case of the Ottine Swamp Monster, it seems as though we might very well be dealing with something far more supernatural than purely physical in nature.

We must then surely wonder: do inter-dimensional beings really exist; creatures that some might call demons, partially-physical entities that only appear in our world at a time and place of their own choosing and desire? Or, could we be dealing with literal animal ghosts in some cases? There is a tale of a ghostly white Bigfoot seen crossing a road near Abilene; so perhaps, some of Texas's monsters are phantoms, or apparitions, as opposed to actual living creatures.

Keeping in this spirit, we conclude with an unearthly account from May of 1913 that didn't surface until 1978, when the last remaining eyewitnesses decided to finally tell his side of the story. The elderly man recalled how he and two other boys were cutting cotton on their farm near Farmersville, north-east of Dallas, when they heard their dogs carrying on. The trio went over to investigate, and were shocked to discover a little, green man, standing only a foot and a half tall.

The witness remembered: "He didn't seem to have on any shoes but I don't really remember his feet. His arms were hanging down just beside him, like they was growed [sic] down the side of him. He had on a kind of hat that reminded me of a Mexican hat. It was a little round hat that looked like it was built onto him. He didn't have on any clothes. Everything looked like a rubber suit including the hat."

In short order, their dogs pounced on the tiny being and begin to rip him to shreds. It was then that the boys could see that its internal organs appeared to look very human-like. It is worth noting that just 16 years prior to this encounter, in 1897, a UFO is said to have crashed only 50 or so miles to the west of Farmersville, near the tiny town of Aurora. Could there possibly be a connection? Was this, perhaps, a little green man from Mars? Real or imagined, one thing is for sure: Texas truly is a land of tall tales and unresolved mysteries.

Before we move on to the next chapter, take a look at the following stories that my co-author, Nick, came across while ferreting in old and dusty media archives, and which relate to some distinctly weird and fringe-like creatures whose existence was reported in the newspapers of old Texas.

First, we have this memorable, yet very odd tale from the *Galveston Daily News* of May 17, 1883: "A reporter observed a photographer this morning, with his battery planted in front of Mr. Baldwin's City Livery stable, on Fannin Street, and immediately went for an item, and got what he went for. The artist was taking the counterfeit presentment of a mule, or jennet that presents a freak of nature, as strange as we ever saw in a menagerie or a museum. It is natural enough in its general build, proportions, and appearances, but its two fore feet are shaped like human feet or rather like a pair of India rubber slippers, and its hind feet are about 18 inches long, and project in a spiral coil, and look like a compromise between a ram's horn and an elephant's trunk. While the reporter was there, Dr. D.F. Stuart came up and examined the animal, and joined in the general idea that it is a strange freak of nature. We understand that the proprietors of several northern museums have written to Mr. Baldwin to know what he will take for his remarkable mule."

Then we have this one, extracted from the pages of the March 24, 1884 edition of the *Galveston Daily News*: "Eagle Pass, 'human deformity', local physician – This curiosity is three days old, weighs five and a half pounds, has a well developed head, but no sign of hair, and when viewing it in a dark room with a lighted lamp it seems to be perfectly transparent, an object on the opposite side of the head being easily distinguished, and what appears to be the brain is constantly moving, not even ceasing when the child appears to be sleeping. The body, as low down to the hips is well developed and symmetrically formed, but the legs, feet, arms and hands have the exact counterparts of the centipede, the fingers and toes resembling the claws of one of those reptiles, and are of a fleshy substance, but have been growing harder ever since birth. The toes and fingers are also transparent, being of a light reddish color, and are ever and often on the move. Should this nondescript live, it will prove to be the greatest curiosity ever known to anatomy."

Also from the *Galveston Daily News* – of May 31, 1884 – is this unusual story: "A natural monstrosity, in the shape of a young calf with seven legs and eight feet, was being exhibited today as a natural curiosity. The animal was born dead several miles from the city."

And then we have yet another from the same newspaper, but dated June 7, 1885: "Mr. W.H. Bailey, of the Herald, has brought to light a strange specimen of malformation. This is his description of it: A most wonderful curiosity in the shape of a pig with a head something like a dog's and a tail resembling that of a horse, was thrown to a reporter of the Herald this morning. This strange monstrosity is about a week old and is in a healthy condition. It belongs to an old colored woman named Martha Simpson, living in the Fourth Ward, south. A number of people visited her house yesterday to get a glimpse of the animal. "

From the *San Antonio Light* of March 20, 1888, we get the following story from Weatherford: "A monstrosity was born in Parker County a few days ago, that seemed to be part pig, part elephant and part human. It only lived a few minutes, but is preserved in alcohol, and can be seen in Weatherford."

Then there is this particularly odd account that was published in the August 2, 1888 edition of the *Galveston Daily News*, and which concerns an event that occurred in the city itself: "A gentleman from the country this morning was exhibiting to curious citizens an odd natural freak in the shape of an opossum of more than usual size, and possessing all the well-defined facial features of an infant. The ears, nose, forehead and chin are well developed and shapely, but the even and symmetrical development of the animal in its alliance to the human family is marred by the member which Darwin credited to our early parents – a tail. Its voice somewhat resembles that of the suppressed sobs of a babe. It is a curious looking creature and will probably be purchased and exhibited by some of our scientific townsmen."

Moving on, consider this, taken from the *Dallas Morning News* of July 20, 1889. Emanating from the town of Hillsboro, it records that: "A physician of this city recently removed a tape worm 40 feet in length from the stomach of a little 3-year-old child of this city. The little one had been in wretched health for some but is now improving rapidly."

Three years later, on July 13, 1892, specifically, the *Galveston Daily News* noted: "A mulatto woman living near here gave birth to a freak resembling a turtle. It is a female about eight inches long and apparently healthy. Its head and face are those of a human being, while the balance of its body is like that of animal. The nails are like claws while the body is covered with hair."

And what are we to make of this eye-opening revelation that was published in the *San Antonio*

Daily Light on April 18, 1894, and that described very high-strangeness in Burton? "News of a strange freak of nature comes from Burton, a small town in the western part of Washington County. Today, a colored woman, attended by Dr. Laas, gave birth to a child, the trunk of which bore a striking resemblance to a red snapper. The lower limbs were perfectly natural and well developed. The attending physician offered a large sum for the specimen, which he desired to preserve but the parents would not let him have it. The colored people who viewed the monstrosity fled in great alarm, and the community is greatly excited over it. They declare the mother to have been hoodooed or conjured."

Galeveston was once again in the news with an eerie tale, on May 13, 1897 specifically, as the *Galeveston Daily News* noted: "A freak of nature from the animal kingdom in the way of a cow with eighteen horns is now on exhibition in Taylor. Ten of her horns measure in varying lengths from ten to twenty inches, representing the horns of the cow, the goat and the sheep, while the eight smallest horns form a representation of the calf, the kid and the lamb. This freak excites considerable curiosity."

Then, we have what is practically a whole series of reports that appeared in the *Dallas Morning News* in 1899. The first, of July 30 of that year, reveals the story of a weird animal seen at Groesbeck, and says: "J.T. Freeman who lives about seven miles west of town on J.C. Sanders' farm, brought into town this morning a freak of nature. It was a pig: the frame was perfect; the head contained no eyes and resembled the head of a human being in shape. The nose was a butt of flabby flesh, but had no nostril. The mouth was as perfect as that of an infant, having the tongue also in its perfectness. The two fore feet were covered with toes, eleven on each foot, resembling the human fingers very much, though they were without nails. The hind feet resembled the human foot, each toe having a perfect nail. The hide or skin covering the body was smooth as that of a human being. The people who witnessed this freak of nature noticed in an instant the resemblance of a human being."

On October 24, 1899, another story of the strange creature surfaced out of Paris, Texas, as the *Dallas Morning News* told its readers: "A sow on the farm of Mr. Argyle Wynne, four miles south-east of Paris, gave birth to a litter of pigs, four of which have snouts like an elephant's trunk growing out of their foreheads and extending down below the nose. Three of the five pigs died in a few hours. The fourth pig lived four days."

Then, barely a couple of weeks later – on November 4, 1899, specifically – the *Dallas Morning News* splashed the following over its packed pages, a story that had burst forth out of Texarkana: "A curiosity was seen on exhibition in this city-today, it being an ox that had one arm projecting from the shoulder blade, about two feet long. The limb has an elbow and a hand containing six claws, all faculties of the member resembling very much those of a human being. The animal belongs to a farmer near this place."

Seventy two hours later, high-strangeness was coming out of Denton – which, as we have noted, is also the reputed home of an infamous Goat Man – as, yet again, the *Dallas Morning News* highlighted: "A mule that would grace a side show on account of its great size was in a local wagon yard today. The animal was certainly a freak as far as size goes, and the head was enormously large even for the great size of the other parts of the body. *The News* correspondent is a half inch over six feet tall, and when he stood by the side of the mule the latter towered above his fully four inches."

And, finally, there's the very brief but interesting story of a horny chicken that became famous in the *Dallas Morning News* issue of May 8, 1903: "Cal Yancy, who lives a little way from Eastland, had on exhibition yesterday a strange freak in the nature of a horned game chicken. The chicken had two horns, one about one and one-quarter of an inch long, and the other about one inch. They were hard and protruded, one over each eye. The chicken was in other respect perfect."

As the newspaper articles related above clearly demonstrate, Texas was home to far more than a few fringe beasts long before anyone could possibly have even guessed!

Chapter X

The Horror of Hecate Hill

(Nick Redfern)

The brainchild of a Dallas, Texas-based author, film-maker and artist named Bill Fountain, *Hecate Hill* is a two-act play that did the rounds in Dallas in late 2006, and that tells the story of a group of friends that head off for a claustrophobic cabin deep in the backwoods of Atoka County, Oklahoma where something large, hairy and violent lurks. Yep: Bigfoot is on the loose and he is not a happy soul; not at all.

It all begins in a bright and breezy fashion as we get to know the lives and loves of the characters – Skim, Blue, Kylie, Maddie, Liver, and Red Death. But, inevitably, that bright and breezy atmosphere, and the joking around are soon replaced by something far more frightening. As the gang settles in, fragmentary reports are picked up on their radio to the effect that a giant, hairy creature has been shot by hunters in Oklahoma and its body is due to be studied by the world's scientific elite. As the night progresses, and the group becomes ever more alarmed by the fact that they are out in the woods in an area known for intense man-beast activity, the story develops rapidly: an announcement is made to the effect that the president is about to make a speech concerning the historic discovery; CNN will be showing the body of the beast on prime-time television; and Bigfoot, so long the subject of derision and ridicule, is about to be unleashed upon an amazed world.

But then, just before the staggering truth can be revealed to one and all, something even stranger happens: all across the world the lights suddenly begin to go out. Engines stop running. Frantic voices report that an "electromagnetic pulse"-type weapon is bringing our civilization to a grinding standstill. And, seemingly out of nowhere, strange "shadow creatures" begin to materialize *en masse* all around the planet. Then there is nothing but complete darkness and never ending radio static. Aside, that is, from the weird, animalistic noises that emanate from the dark woods and that reverberate around the cabin.

Bigfoot, it seems, is not the large and lumbering ape that many assume it to be, after all. Rather, it is the denizen of another dimension – a realm that co-exists with ours and where time, as we understand at least, is barely a relevant factor. The killing of one of its kind duly leads the creatures to launch an all-out planetary assault and we, the Human Race, are soon reduced to – as the publicity blurb for the play puts it – "the bottom of the food chain."

As the nightmarish night progresses, and as the menacing growls get ever closer to the cabin and a thunderous storm of almost apocalyptic levels grows, tensions among certain elements of the group increase until they reach levels of literal terror. But, by now, some of the friends are not so sure that anything untoward has taken place at all – that is, other than an immense and ingenious practical joke perpetrated by the character Blue. Is the end really nigh for planet earth? Or is this merely Blue's own, unique, and brilliantly-executed, homage to Orson Welles' infamous, hysteria-inducing radio production of H. G. Wells' *War of the Worlds*? Indeed, one character proclaims loudly: "This is a really stupid way for the world to end!" And, thus, their – and our – suspicions are reinforced that perhaps all is not quite as it seems. Or is it?

Ken and I will not spoil the ending for those that may want to catch *Hecate Hill* for themselves. But it should be noted that this is a story that grips right to the very last scene and remains thought-provoking throughout. Taking nods from Sam Raimi's cult classic film, *The Evil Dead*, and the aforementioned *War of the Worlds*, *Hecate Hill* is an atmospheric production with a writer, cast and crew that have worked hard to create a story about Bigfoot that does not follow accepted convention and wisdom. And talking of the writer, Dallas's Bill Fountain elaborated to me in late 2006 – and just over the road from the monster-infested White Rock Lake, in fact – on what it was that prompted him to produce write and produce *Hecate Hill*:

"All of my life I've been fascinated with the notion of Bigfoot. As a little kid, I remember my great-grandmother in Oklahoma would tell me stories about these giant skunk-apes. She could tell great ghost stories. As a kid, anytime there was a documentary, or pseudo-documentary, on TV I was there. There was always that thing about how something that big couldn't exist. But then another part of me was like: 'Please let it be true.'"

It seems that, consciously or not, some of Fountain's views on Bigfoot and the paranormal had their origins in a strange incident that occurred in his childhood. He says: "I'll never forget when I was a little kid I saw a very bizarre thing that I could not explain, and to this day I have no idea what it meant. I was about five years old. I was outside; it was dusk, and the trees were swaying with a storm coming. I saw what looked like some kind of a weird, horned thing with these big red eyes, sticking a hand down out of a cloud behind the trees. It saw me and it looked right at me. Then, it was like it pulled the cloud up over its face, and it was gone. I ran inside screaming: 'There's a thing in the cloud!' Very much like a gargoyle. I've thought since: What was it? Was it an over-active imagination? Did I not get enough sleep? Who knows?"

Fountain added to me: 'That incident has become a strong thread through some of my writing

Courtesy: Level Ground Arts / Bill Fountain

Above: Bill Fountain, the writer of Hecate Hill (Level Ground Arts / Bill Fountain)
Below: The cast (Bill Fountain)

– the idea that there are these shadow-things that move in-between worlds. I remember from that incident the sensation of being alone in the woods, in the dark, hearing a noise, and being scared out of my mind. And I wanted to write a play about that sensation. That's what I tried to do.

"And," he said, not without some justification, as we sat and chatted: "Bigfoot gets a lot of bad press too. There's a lot of goofy stuff – *Harry and the Hendersons*. Bigfoot's very funny and it's a great joke until you're in the woods and it's dark and something makes a noise. Then, it's not a joke anymore. And I thought: wouldn't it be cool if someone put something together that captured that?"

Fountain continued: "I also wanted the audience to think about questions like: How well do you know your friends? How much would you trust your friends in a situation like this? And at what point do you throw it out and say: 'This cannot be a joke.' That's what it's really about."

Whatever the true nature of Bigfoot, Fountain believes it to be more than just mere flesh and blood in nature and origin: "I have always thought that if there was a creature like that, it would have to be something that could kind of drift in and out of our reality. It's funny because after I wrote the play I was watching a show about Native American legends about Bigfoot and they have very much that dream-state approach to Bigfoot. It's something, I think, that's in the peripheral of our reality: a shadow-creature."

And, in a very synchronistic fashion that would surely have made the late John Keel nod sagely and knowingly, Fountain revealed to me that: "One weird thing is that when I was writing *Hecate Hill* I wanted to be very specific about the location of the story; so I looked at a map and picked Atoka County, Oklahoma. Then, less than four weeks after we first said we were going to put on the production, there was a rash of Bigfoot sightings not far from where I had set the story. This was pretty weird and scary; like life imitating art and coming true."

And the big screen may be looming, too for North America's most famous man-beast: "We want to do a *Hecate Hill* film; an independent feature film," explained Fountain, as I listened carefully. "I've done a lot of short films, but this will be my first feature-length production. We'll use the same cast and I'd like to start it in the spring. And I want to put out a graphic novel, too, that follows what happens to one of the characters in the stage production."

Interestingly, Fountain says: "I was shocked at how easily my family and friends all accepted *Hecate Hill*. The thing that knocked me out was that when you mention Bigfoot, suddenly there's interest. So many people are totally enamored and fascinated with it. Everyone has an opinion about what Bigfoot is."

Also looming for Fountain is a stage version of one of the creepiest films ever made: *Carnival of Souls*. Fountain took up the story: "The first time I saw that film it disturbed me on a fundamental level. I first saw it as a kid and every couple of years I'll watch it again, and I've always wanted to turn it into a stage play. But in doing so I had a tremendous amount of respect for what they did with the original and I didn't want to duplicate that. But, I had been watching a lot of footage of the Hurricane Katrina victims in New Orleans. And I started thinking about how a lot of those hurricane victims were stuck in a limbo, a purgatory, like the character in the film. So, I have an idea to put that sense of purgatory into a New Orleans setting: purgatory, with one-part voodoo and one-part Catholicism."

Indeed, Fountain has a finger in numerous pies: in 2005 he put out a graphic novel based on Edgar Allen Poe's *The Raven*, and he's also working on his own version of *War of the Worlds* for Texas's Mesquite Community Theatre. As he puts it: "I work in whatever medium tells the story the best. I love the immediacy and intensity of theatre, and that instant rapport with the audience is incredible. But I think there's room open for everything – theatre, graphic-novel, and film."

As we rounded matters up, Fountain said: "I like to think that everything I do has some sort of purpose beyond that of just simple entertainment; that everything I do has a point. Whether or not that point is communicated depends on the audience, of course. But I hope that people can come away having learned something. And I love to tell a good story, of course. People can say there has never been a Bigfoot, but we just don't know. What if there are these incredible creatures out there? And it can go the other way, too: how much do you know about your friends? How much do we know about anything? Those are the questions that *Hecate Hill* asks."

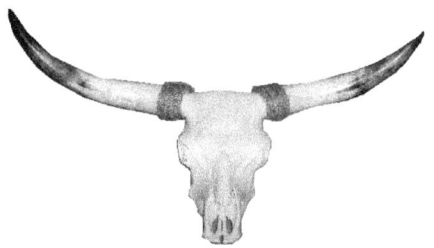

Chapter XI
Out-of-place Animals
By Ken Gerhard

Reports of big, mysterious cats – often referred to as black panthers – turn up on a very regular basis at various places throughout Europe and North America. These animals have been linked to heinous livestock killings and are usually feared, due to their size and ferocity. A number of such panther reports have been logged in Texas, where the mountain lion and the bobcat are the largest feline species currently recognized by local wildlife officials. Black coloration – or the genetic condition known as melanism – is rare in wild cats, but is most common in the leopard of Africa and Asia, as well as in the jaguar of Central and South America.

The North American mountain lion or cougar, typically, possesses a tan or cream-colored coat; no authenticated cases of black specimens have ever been documented, thus far at least. While some bobcats can appear dark in color, they rarely weigh more than 30 pounds, hardly big enough to inspire any degree of awe or fear. The jaguar's range does extend into parts of Mexico and it's not impossible that a few might just occasionally wander into Texas from time to time.

There is even an account from 1946, which tells of a jaguar being killed near Brownsville. But, black jaguars are not known to exist north of Panama – only spotted ones. Thus, the possibility of black jaguars wandering around Texas seems highly unlikely. Still, Texans from the deserts of the south-west to the eastern bottomlands have described encountering exceptionally large, black felines slinking along the edge of humanity.

There is, for example, a dramatic account from September 17, 1881 that tells of two loggers named Alfred Creswell and Henry Winters, who were attacked by a pair of panthers while walking along a railroad track near Lumberton, in south-east Texas. The men were eventually able to fend off their attackers by yielding large sticks, although the assault lasted for almost half an hour. At some point, the big cats gave up and the men were very lucky indeed to escape with only deep scratches and torn clothing.

Another black panther may have been killed in 1897 by a man named Robert Jordan, a passenger traveling down the Sabine River on the steamer *R.E. Lee*. Jordan had spotted the creature hiding in a tree. He apparently shot the animal and then had it mounted and placed in the ship's wheelhouse, although there is no record of what ultimately became of the near unique specimen.

In recent years, Ryan and Lisa Knott, who publish a weekly newspaper in Warren, Texas, wrote that they had a family of black panthers living behind their property in the midst of the Big Thicket. The Knotts described how the big cats would roam a dirt road by their house at night, leaving behind classic tell-tale cat-like tracks. The family would also hear screams on occasion, and one time their Great Dane almost got into it with one of the creatures. Nearby, in Orange County, a Mr. Chaisson claimed that he once saw a black panther, accompanied by two cubs no less, at a place called Cow Bayou.

During the early part of 2007, north-east Texas was the site of an absolute rash of big cat sightings. First, residents in Dialville, located in Cherokee County near Nacogdoches, began to report seeing an apparently fully-grown black panther, accompanied by three juveniles, stalking the area around County Road 1610. Officials from the Texas Parks and Wildlife Department quickly debunked the claims, stating that the culprits were more than likely bobcats, or perhaps even large house cats.

Within days, there were sightings of a panther only 40 miles to the north in Upshur County, at a place called Raintree Lake. Local rancher Wayne Ballad discovered that one of his calves had been killed, with its throat and stomach ripped open by some unknown predator-like beast. In addition, one of Ballard's neighbors had noticed that several dogs had gone missing in recent weeks, and many people in the area had heard a sound like a woman screaming at night. Eyewitness Mitchell Bransford claimed to have had two or three close encounters with the creature, causing him to have distinct chills. He described it as looking like: "A big, black panther." He added that: "I'm not talking about a glance. I'm talking straight at him and him just looking at me."

Dr. Karl Shuker is one of the world's foremost authorities on cryptid cats. He feels that most sightings of so-called black panthers are probably misidentifications of known species. For example, a mountain lion with a wet coat could appear to be dark-colored, especially at night. As we've suggested, there are dark gray and brown-colored bobcats in Texas, and people unfamiliar with them could indeed quite easily misjudge their size and color from a distance. There is also the enigmatic Jaguarundi, a fair-sized, strange-looking cat that is occasionally native to the Rio Grande Valley.

In addition to wild cats, there could be misidentifications of black house cats muddling the mystery. The gene, which causes domestic cats to be melanistic in color, also tends to make them grow somewhat bigger than normal. So, in some respects, big, black tomcats could, po-

Beware the mysterious cats of Texas (Nick Redfern)

Texas cats past and present: Bobcat (above) are still found quite commonly whereas pumas (below) are presumed extinct, although the odd sighting suggests that they linger on (CFZ)

tentially at least, be to blame. Shuker sensibly points out that, in a number of cases, people may actually be seeing black leopards that have perhaps escaped, or that may even have been released into the wild by negligent owners. Apparently, black leopards are a very popular breed with big cat collectors. All of these factors could be combining to compound the mystery of the inexplicable black panthers of Texas.

In early 2009, Nick Redfern spent several days delving deeply into the old archives of a variety of Texas-based newspapers, and uncovered a number of significant reports from years past of big cats on the loose in Texas. For example, on July 11, 1880, the *Dallas Morning News* reported that in the vicinity of Whitewright: "...A puma which has been infesting the neighborhood of Pilot Grove for several weeks yesterday tore to pieces and devoured the two-year-old child of a farmer living on the Burns tract. Nothing was left of the child by the beast but the fleshless bones. The puma has been seen several times in North Texas."

Then there is the following, very brief, account that was published in the March 14, 1896 issue of the *Dallas Morning News*. Detailing the killing of a big cat in Denison, it states: "Tom Crowder of Pottsboro captured a monster wildcat in the bottoms. The cat measured five feet two inches from tip to tip."

Then, there are the following reports Nick uncovered that relate to a spate of big cat attacks around San Antonio in January 1900. According to the *San Antonio Daily Light* newspaper of January 8: "Some ferocious wild beast, believed to have been either a wild cat, panther * or Mexican lion **, attacked a cow belonging to a man named Wander, on Leal Street yesterday morning at 10 o'clock and bit the animal several times in the neck. It was frightened off, however, before the cow was killed. The cow has since died. Her calf which she was defending was killed."

On the following day – January 9 – the *Galveston Daily News* reported that: "A posse of citizens, headed by the assistant chief of police of San Antonio, the other day chased a panther which had for some time been lurking in the suburbs of the city and depredating in chicken coops. They failed to catch him, having lost the trail in the chaparral, only three miles from the center of the city. This was not the panther which Mr. Bryan and the citizens ran into a tree and captured alive. The San Antonio panther was wild."

The *San Antonio Light* newspaper noted on the same day: "The capture of the bobtailed wild cat on the Leona Sunday afternoon has not served to make the residents of the west-side rest easy, as it did not rid them of the animal that had recently been disturbing their chicken coops and cow pens.

"As mentioned yesterday, the beast attacked and killed a cow on Leona Street Sunday night

---

** Panther and Mexican Lion both presumably refer to the puma *(P. concolor)* although it is intriguing that they are referred to as different animals. The North American lion *(Panthera leo atrox)* was the largest big cat ever to have existed and became extinct only 11,000 years ago - a mere bagatelle in evolutionary terms. Could it have survived to the present day? Various people have suggested just that!

and it was back in the same community last night. About 9.30 o'clock it was seen in the rear yard of the Murphy residence on Rusi Street, and was chased back to Leal Street through the yard of Mr. Wander where it killed the cow the night previous. Here it was almost overtaken by the pursuers – George Rine and Walter O'Brient – and both fired at it; one with a revolver and one with a shotgun but with a howl of rage or pain as if shot, it bounded away and escaped.

"The boys had a good look at it, and it was larger than the wild-cats killed Sunday, which lends to the belief that it is a panther as was at first supposed. The beast is believed to have remained in the vicinity and continued his prowl during the rest of the night, as fowls were heard making a noise as if disturbed suddenly in various parts of the community the remainder of the night."

One further story that Nick found originated in Calvert, and was related within the pages of the February 16, 1903 edition of the *Dallas Morning News*. It reads thus: "From Alderman C.S. Allen, *The News* correspondent, learns of the story of a thrilling adventure with a Mexican lion a night or so ago in North Calvert. Alderman Allen states the beast had been prowling around in his neighborhood for several nights, playing sad havoc with the chickens, until he drifted into the yard of Lee Horton, who owns two large bull dogs. The dogs attacked the lion and a fierce fight followed, when Mr. Horton appeared on the scene with a shotgun and riddled the ferocious animal with buckshot, but not until the beast had almost killed one of the dogs. Just where the animal came from is a mystery. He is described as a large, ferocious animal, and was evidently driven into town by intense hunger."

While investigating the Coleman Critter – a so-called Chupacabras that was shot in central Texas during 2005 – I heard locals reference another shooting near Coleman, which evidently involved a perplexed hunter and a strangely out-of-place monkey. The incident, as well as a photo of the dead monkey at issue, had graced the cover of the local newspaper and led to quite an uproar in the animal rights community around the country. At first, I was at a complete loss to understand how on earth a monkey could possibly be running around in the middle of Texas, although the obvious assumption would be that perhaps it had escaped from some sort of collector or from a traveling circus. However, I later learned that Frio County in south Texas is, in fact, home to a population of several hundred monkeys, due to an experiment that has most definitely gone more than a tad awry.

In 1972, a group of about 150 Japanese snow monkeys, more properly referred to as Japanese macaques *(Macaca fuscata)*, were relocated from the suburbs of Kyoto, Japan, to a primate sanctuary near Dilley, Texas. The mischievous macaques had apparently worn out their welcome in Kyoto. To the surprise of just about everyone involved, the monkeys adapted well to their new environment and within two decades, their population had multiplied to nearly 600 individuals. The enterprising snow monkeys eventually figured out how to supersede the confines of their security fences and, subsequently, began to trespass on the neighboring ranches and adjoining properties. As some ranchers began to complain that the primates were becoming an absolute nuisance, the subject of whether or not the monkeys were, or indeed should be, on the protected species list was hotly debated. Gun-toting fanatics soon began seeking permits to hunt the feral macaques, resulting in three monkeys being tragically and needlessly shot near the end of the 1995 hunting season. Today, the snow monkey population lives happily and contentedly within the confines of a new facility with far better security, although it's not impossible that a few crafty individuals may still manage to escape from time to time.

Since the great state of Texas has played, and continues to play, host to many exotic hunting reserves and menageries, there have been instances where escapes by, or releases of, non-native species have occurred. As a result, there are countless stories from local outdoorsmen who have come across animals that seem to be very out-of-place indeed.

A fly fishing guide once told me, quite seriously, that he came face-to-face with an African antelope in the Texas hill country. And who can say otherwise? In addition, cryptozoologist Chester Moore Jr. captured a photo of a white elk wandering in front of his camera trap in east Texas. On another one of his cameras, Chester secured an image of a creature which bears a very striking resemblance to the red wolf (*Canis rufus*), which is now officially considered to be wholly extinct within the state of Texas. I, myself, think I might well have spotted a red wolf near El Campo five years ago. So, perhaps, their extinction here is a wholly false presumption. Texas is, after all, a very big state indeed, and one with plenty of dark and secure places to hide.

My absolute favorite story about a weird, out-of-place animal involves an escaped African monitor lizard, which had taken up residence under a house in my old downtown Houston neighborhood during the 1980s. Residents in the area had been noticing that the neighborhood cats had been mysteriously disappearing for years. When the five foot long lizard was finally discovered, its underground lair was apparently littered with the bones of its unfortunate feline victims.

Speaking of large reptiles, a 13 foot alligator was shot by game wardens in West Columbia, Texas on April 16, 2005, after homeowners Anita and Charles Rogers called to report that a gigantic alligator was swimming around in the bayou behind their house. Their friends in the Bar X neighborhood had also encountered it and the Rogers could hear a loud bellowing noise at night. A photo of the dead creature was posted on the internet and was subsequently seen by many people, although the size of the gator was often exaggerated – as, it must be admitted, often occurs in such cases. Still, having grown up canoeing the bayous near West Columbia, I find this monster story particularly appealing. And, back in April of 1977, a strangely out-of-place, 700 pound alligator was found in a shallow creek near Junction, Texas on the edge of what is a virtual desert.

A humorous incident involving an escaped, red kangaroo took place in the city of Lewisville Texas, during December of 2007. Veterinarian Kyle Jones of the Southridge Animal Hospital had taken the ill marsupial (named Maynard) home with him, so that he could nurse it back to health. One day, at around four in the afternoon, Jones was putting up his Christmas tree lights when Maynard, who had been contentedly and blissfully grazing in the yard, suddenly bolted out a wooden, fenced gate that had been blown open by the wind.

For 20 minutes or so, amazed, amused and bemused neighbors watched in complete and utter disbelief as the three foot tall, 60 pound kangaroo wildly hopped around the neighborhood at speeds sometimes approaching 25 miles per hour. Police officers who were dispatched to the scene attempted to corral the elusive animal, and in a fashion that must have surely rivaled some of the classic *Keystone Cops* films of decades ago.

Finally, motorcycle officer Scott Hayney managed to grab an exhausted Maynard by the tail, while the creature was attempting to scoot between his legs. Local officials ultimately and sternly ruled that a kangaroo had no place at all in Lewisville, and urged Jones to find a zoo that would take the animal. Fortunately, no charges were filed against Dr. Jones – or against Maynard, I am very pleased to report.

Not quite as weird, but certainly worth mentioning, are the recurring appearances of manatees in Texas waters. West Indian manatees also, known as sea cows, are primarily native to the warm coastal marshes of the Gulf Coast. They can be found around Mexico's Yucatan Peninsula, the Caribbean, and also in the rivers and waterways of Florida and Georgia. Sea cows are truly enormous, aquatic mammals that can reach lengths of up to ten feet and can often weigh in at an impressive 1,200 pounds, though they are typically docile, slow-moving vegetarians. One theory holds that they might have shared a common ancestor with elephants. Their range may have extended into Texas in the past, but now the waters of the northern Gulf are generally considered to be far too cold for these animals to survive and thrive with any firm degree of success.

Occasionally, however, rogue specimens are discovered in the Lone Star State. As a perfect example of this, on March 28, 1902, the *Dallas Morning News* reported the following from Corpus Christi: "The first manatee, or sea hog, ever captured in Corpus Christi waters has been on exhibition here all day. The monster was caught today by a local showman, but died after being taken from the water. Old fishermen say they never before heard of a sea hog captured on the Texas coast."

Moving on nearly a century, during 1996, for example, an eight foot long female (nicknamed Sweet Pea), was found near a wastewater plant in Houston's Buffalo Bayou. No-one was quite sure how the mysterious manatee ended up there. But, for a while at least, local officials took careful measures to feed and protect the animal, while curious onlookers from around the city showed up in absolute droves to gawk at the strange, out-of-place creature.

Eventually, a 240 pound net was flown in from Florida and a rescue mission was mounted to extract Sweet Pea from the bayou's frigid waters. After a short recovery at San Antonio's *Sea World*, the misplaced manatee was tagged and transported back to Florida for release back into the wild.

Similarly, on June 3, 2007 a sickly sea cow nicknamed Texas was discovered near an industrial pipe outflow off the coast of Corpus Christi. The distressed animal was suffering from symptoms similar to frostbite, but was successfully rescued by wildlife workers, who transported the manatee to a facility for rehabilitation. Poor Texas was eventually returned to full health and successfully released into Florida's Crystal River.

When discussing absurd animals in Texas, we must not neglect to mention the fabulously ridiculous Jackalope, an imaginary creature whose image adorns various souvenir shops throughout the state. Many Texans own mock taxidermy style Jackalope heads, and have them mounted on the walls in their homes. Jackalopes are typically portrayed as having the body of a jackrabbit, but with antelope horns attached to their heads. The origin of these fanciful critters can be traced back to the state of Wyoming, decades ago, and has ever since been sustained by Texas taxidermists with a distinct sense of humor.

Texans have also adopted the fabricated Jackalope as a state symbol, and understandably so too. The mythological beast, with its imaginary attributes, greatly exemplifies our attitudes toward this vast and mysterious state. We like to think that somewhere out there, hiding behind the tall cactus and countless tumbleweeds, is something legendary and monstrous, just waiting to be discovered. These are the things from which tall tales are truly born.

Nick with Bigfoot researcher Bob Gimlin (Nick Redfern)

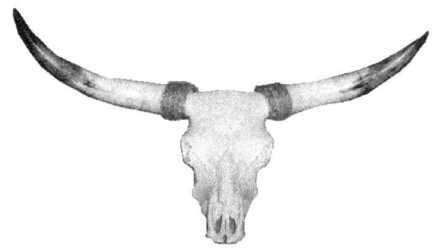

Chapter XII
Bigfoot – East Texan-Style
(Ken Gerhard)

While driving the 850 mile span from El Paso to Orange, it becomes readily apparent to one and all that the great state of Texas is home to a truly massive and diverse range of habitats. Beginning with desert, you will traverse hills, plains, forests and in the end, swampy bottomlands that easily rival the most impenetrable of all jungles. It is within these mysterious marshes that people claim to have had encounters with man-like monsters, which seem to eerily resemble the legendary hairy mountain giants of the Pacific north-west known as Bigfoot. Described as standing seven to nine feet tall, completely covered in hair and emitting a truly foul odor, they are frequently assigned physical attributes of both apes and men.

In Florida's swamps, sightings of similar creatures, known amongst the populace as Skunk Apes, have been documented for absolute decades. As we might expect, stories of these so-called swamp apes, wooly boogers and wild men extend throughout the bottomlands of the south-eastern United States. Like other indigenous peoples in the Americas, the Caddo tribe of east Texas, have ancient legends which tell of tall, hairy beings that live deep in the heart of the woods. And, with literally millions of acres of dense forestland in east Texas, it isn't totally beyond the realm of possibility that these elusive giants could remain hidden from us… lurking just beyond the shadows, and largely surfacing by night to both prowl and feed.

One of the earliest accounts to be published in Texas involves the so-called Cypress Swamp Monster, also referred to as the Caddo Critter. The monster has been making the news around Marion and Harrison Counties in the far north-east corner of the state since 1965. It was on August 20 of that year that 13 year old Johnny Maples was walking home from a friend's house. It was a normal day; for a while, at least. Johnny was on FM 1784, between Prospect and Lodi, when he began to hear noises emanating from the adjacent bushes. He called out twice, thinking that perhaps it was someone he knew from the area. When there was no reply, Johnny became concerned, and picked up a couple of rocks and hurled them into the brush.

"That's when, this large, hairy man or beast appeared near the fence," he recalled. As the frightened boy began running away down the road – even removing his shoes to run ever-faster – the creature climbed over the fence and began to give chase.

"I ran as hard and fast as I could, but he kept up with me and he wasn't running, either, just sort of walking along behind me," Maples remarked. "The last time I turned around, the beast had gone off the road and disappeared into the woods." When young Johnny finally made it home, his mother found him in a distinct state of shock, with a pair of very badly blistered feet. His description of the monster was as follows: "About seven feet tall with thick, long black hair all over its body, except for the face, stomach and palms of its hands."

Caddo Lake on the border of Louisiana has a rich history of encounters with the so-called Caddo Critter. The lake was, in fact, both the location of, and the inspiration for, a B-horror movie titled, *The Creature from Black Lake*, about a violent, killer Bigfoot. A swampy, sinister and very foreboding place indeed, the lake seems like the perfect address where one might find a reclusive monster. It is connected to the system of waterways that leads to Boggy Creek and Fouke, Arkansas, home of the Fouke monster, and the subject of the cult classic, and near-legendary, film, *The Legend of Boggy Creek*. Just a bit south of Caddo Lake, in Harrison County, lies the town of Hallsville, near Longview. During the summer of 1976, there was an intriguing report from Hallsville, which told of two Bigfoot creatures that were apparently traveling together. One of them was described as having white hair and standing an unbelievable 12 feet tall. Its partner appeared to be female and was shorter, with reddish hair. The beings were apparently observed standing in a cornfield while happily shucking corn!

During 1969, the biologist and cryptozoological researcher Ivan Sanderson received a letter from a college student named Thomas R. Adams who attempted to sum up the state of affairs in north-east Texas as it related to unknown animals. Adams wrote thus to Sanderson: "I have no way of knowing how much you know, if any, about the monster situation here in northern Texas. There are several points in this area: an ape-shaped animal that became known as the Critter was seen in the area three or four years ago. A rancher named Charlie Gantt, who fired 10 shots unsuccessfully at the Critter, described it as being seven feet tall and four feet wide and covered with hair."

The letter writer continued: "The residents here claim that the 'Haskell Rascal' and the 'Caddo Critter' are one and the same. Although the Haskell creature has been reported for 80 years… It prowls in the lowlands during the winter, killing and feeding on livestock… The Rascal is also reported to wander throughout a 60-mile range."

Adams also mentioned the region adjacent to the Oklahoma border near Paris, Texas, which traditionally has produced a large amount of Bigfoot activity. He stated: "The Direct vicinity, in extreme north-western Lamar County… The residents of this rural area report what they refer to as the 'Manimal' that makes scheduled appearances in June and October as it migrates through the area. They have reported that it has been seen regularly for the past decade and some old-timers claim that have seen such a thing for the past 50 years… the opinion of most of the residents appears to be, it's real. Descriptions have the creature being about 6' 2" as it stood up. It also has been seen on all fours. Several witnesses have reported that it made 8-foot leaps. It has prowled in the vicinity of houses and has been reported looking in windows. Several years ago a game warden was called to take a look at the tracks. He said the tracks were like nothing he had ever seen."

Just 60 miles south of Paris, many sightings have been logged around the South Sulfur River area, near Commerce. During the summer of 1969, several men, including Jerry Matlock and Kenneth Wilson, encountered an eight foot tall brown-colored Bigfoot with wide shoulders. They all watched it jump over a levee and run right towards their vehicle. The men fired several gunshots at the monster, but all apparently missed. Interestingly, this was the very same time period that saw the Goat Man of Lake Worth rear its pug-ugly head from out of the lake's darkened woods.

Over the course of the next several years, the region would continue to produce consistent reports of a very similar nature. In September of 1973, for example, there were two sightings near Peerless, Texas, and further south near Corsicana, in 1977 there were two, separate Bigfoot encounters reported by wide-eyed motorists.

A weird chain of events took place in the town of Vidor, near Beaumont, far to the south-east. On June 19, 1978, Bobby Bussinger, along with his young wife Beckie, decided to confront whatever had been "clawing at their window screens", as well as making howling and yelping noises throughout the night. The previous evening, things had come to a head when three of their dogs had been killed by the frightening prowler, and a huge commotion broke out in the family's yard.

Something both big and powerful was banging on the walls of their home and tearing the screens off their windows. Bobby, very wisely, reportedly grabbed a shotgun and headed outside to confront whatever was doing it. According to a local newspaper report, he came face to face with: "An erect form, described as taller than 6 feet, with long, shaggy hair and muscular arms that did not scare."

As the creature charged at him, Bobby fired off a round and retreated to the safety of his domicile. That's when Sheriff Jack Reeves was called out to investigate. The Bussingers told the Sheriff all about the strange goings-on, including the discovery of a mysterious lean-to made out of tree limbs that Beckie had observed at the edge of their property. Upon inspection of their home, some of the window frames had indeed been completely broken apart by something unknown. Sheriff Reeves staked out the area that night in his patrol car and spotted a large form lurking about 50 yards away in the shadows, right about the time the noises resumed. That was apparently the final straw for Bobby and Beckie, who immediately packed up their belongings, and moved out of the house forever. The Bussingers described whatever had been terrorizing them as a kind of werewolf.

It just so happened that during February of 2009, I was contacted by one of Texas's top paranormal research groups, which had been investigating possible poltergeist activity at a property in Vidor. The head of the group, Pete Haviland, asked me if a Bigfoot creature might be behind the mysterious events, since residents were reporting bad smells, weird sounds and banging noises on the walls of their trailer at night. In addition, one resident had seen a dark dog-like animal that seemed to vanish into thin air, and another had chased something large into the nearby woods. When the man returned home, his clothes were torn and he was bloody. He appeared to be in shock, and was ranting about how the thing had attacked him.

When I was able to revisit the Bussinger affair, I was intrigued by the similarities between the two cases. Most compelling was the fact that the two locations were only a couple of miles apart: in a very rural setting and with a great deal of wilderness nearby. I decided to travel out to Vidor and join Pete and his group, the *Lone Star Spirits*, for a weekend of investigations.

First, I visited the residence where the Bussingers had been chased from their home, and noticed two people working on a truck in the driveway. I greeted them and approached cautiously, since I did not want to come off as a complete whack-job. The younger of the two, a man in his early twenties, acknowledged me as I walked up the drive, and as I politely explained the purpose of my visit. The older person then came over. It was a woman, who told me that she was, in fact, Beckie Bussinger's older sister and that she now resided there. Beckie's sister explained to me that the so-called creature had in actuality been a human relative, who was strung out on the drug PCP at the time and consequently had reverted to acting like an animal and taking refuge in the nearby woods. She also quipped that if anyone had taken a shotgun to confront the alleged wild man, it probably would have been Beckie and not Bobby! I found no reason why the woman would find it necessary to besmirch her family in any way, shape or form, but I didn't ask why the newspaper's description of the beast indicated that it was some kind of monster, rather than a deranged human.

Meanwhile, as we investigated the then-recent activities at the other property with Pete's group, we discovered a very curious footprint, as well as a lean-to structure in the adjacent woods. Later that night, we heard some wood knocking sounds nearby, which are very often associated with Bigfoot activity.

Throughout my years of investigations, I have interviewed several Texans who have looked me squarely in my eye and told me that they have seen something which could only be described as Bigfoot. A perfect case in point: the illuminating story of Shawn Gregory of Livingston, who grew up near Palestine, in the eastern part of the state. Shawn told me of a remarkable encounter that he had as a boy during the 1980s. He and two friends were riding their bicycles through the woods one day when they suddenly came face to face with a large, human-like monster.

According to Shawn, the being had a man's face, though much wider, and its body was covered in rust-colored hair. The creature stood and stared at the youths for several minutes, continually opening its mouth and exposing its large teeth to them – which was not a good sign, one presumes. At one point, one of Shawn's friends became faint and dropped to his knees.

Eventually, the frightening looking being shuffled off into the forest and disappeared from sight. Yet another eyewitness told me about how he had been hunting near Centerville, which lies halfway between Dallas and Houston, when three, unbelievably-tall humanoid beings walked past the deer blind that he was sitting in. The hunter was absolutely positive that they were not human.

During 1996, a controversial film that alleged to portray Bigfoot was broadcast as part of the television series *Strange Universe*. The footage was reportedly shot by a man named Danny Sweeten in the Sam Houston National Forest near Cleveland, Texas. Sweeten had claimed that he was surveying some property with a video camera in hand, when he suddenly walked upon a seven foot tall man-like animal lounging on the ground.

According to Sweeten, after a brief staring contest, the creature rose to its feet and struck him in his chest, knocking him to the ground and even loosening some of his teeth. As the man-monster retreated into the depths of the pine thicket, he managed to videotape it, with the resulting footage revealing a tall hairy figure with a cone-shaped head walking swiftly behind some trees. Sweeten described his attacker as having thin patchy hair and a face that appeared to hang low. At first, the footage looked convincing to some investigators, but then inaccuracies began to surface in Sweeten's testimony.

A few months later, Danny produced another so-called Bigfoot video that involved a comical-looking figure parading into view near an undisclosed wooded area. Sweeten also alleged to have audio recordings of the Bigfoot, which sounded suspiciously like a deer-call being blown into a bucket. Physical anthropologist Dr. Grover Krantz analyzed the first film Sweeten made and dismissed it as a fake, since the subject had an obvious man-like gait and appeared to be a human wearing a costume.

Despite the controversial nature of the story related directly above, it's important to note that my own personal forays into south Texas's Big Thicket National Preserve have left me somewhat convinced, at least, that unknown, ape-like creatures could indeed lurk within its swampy confines. The Thicket boasts almost 100,000 acres of dense, impassible woodland and is very well-known for its abundant wildlife and mysterious stories of ghost lights, big cats and wild men.

On one of my first expeditions there, I discovered an inexplicable hut-like structure at a place called Turkey Creek. Similar structures have been found in other areas around the country, including Ohio and Florida and are believed to have been constructed by Bigfoot-style creatures. The hut seemed to be woven together with saplings that were bent over to form a very intricate foundation. The top was thatched with dry grass and leaves, and the opening seemed big enough to accommodate a large animal; although I doubt any human would dare to enter into its snake-friendly interior. Nearby, I found a thick branch that had literally been corkscrewed and pulled across the trail – yet another potentially-classic sign of definitive Bigfoot habitation.

The most dramatic evidence that I have personally experienced with regards to these creatures occurred during 2003, at Little Cottonwood Lake in the northern-most part of the state. Researcher Chester Moore Jr. and I were at the remote location in the Caddo Grasslands, investigating reports of a monster that had been chasing campers out of the woods. It was just after dark when we struck out to hike the perimeter of the lake. Almost immediately, we began to hear loud grunting sounds that reminded us of someone, or something, extremely large, laughing or panting. Chester and I were both in agreement that it was not any Texas animal that we had ever previously heard in the North American outdoors.

In fact, it reminded me most of all of the Howler Monkeys that I had previously heard down in Central America, or perhaps gorillas that I had heard at the zoo. The sounds were emanating from some brush near the lake and seemed very close... perhaps a little too close for comfort, even. Fortunately, I had my camcorder running at the time and was able to capture the hair-raising vocalizations on tape for posterity.

A short while later, while perched on a levy overlooking the lake, we could see two greenish-yellow eyes reflecting in our spotlights in the exact location where we had heard the sounds. The eyes seemed to be far too high off the ground to belong to a deer or to any other type of known animal. The following morning, while I was exploring the spot where we had heard the noises, I stumbled upon a small beach that was littered with the shells of dead turtles. Strangely and eerily, their shells had been ripped in two; all of their flesh was gone.

A flurry of reports relating to a being known as the Monkey Man erupted in the south-east Texas town of Dayton during the summer of 2003. The encounters came to full prominence in July of that year, when residents started to write to the local newspaper, which in turn found that sheriff's deputies had, in fact, already been looking into the sightings for some time.

The animal was described as being somewhat short and stocky, with reddish hair, about five feet tall and possessing the general form of a monkey, but standing upright like a man. It was most often seen along the Trinity River near FM 1409 and Country Road 455. One resident even watched the Monkey Man jump off the roof of his house one evening. People from Dayton began to recall a monster known as the Day Lakes Goat Man that had been seen by teenagers in the same area, years earlier. One man wrote to the newspaper to say that he had been bow-hunting at Day Lake when he spotted something that looked like a hog running around on its hind legs. Goat Men and bipedal pigs aside there is ample evidence indicating that man-like apes, known as Bigfoot, are indeed roaming the forests of eastern Texas.

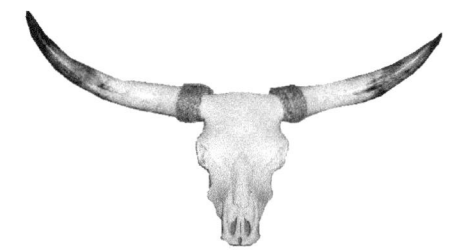

CONCLUSIONS

And now, dear readers, our long, winding and beastly saga is finally at an end. We hope that the many and varied tales, stories and legends of Bigfoot, the Chupacabras, lake monsters, werewolves, giant winged beasts, wild men of the woods, gargoyles, the Goat Man and much more of a monstrous nature in the Lone Star State have entertained you, enthralled you, intrigued you, and perhaps even frightened you, too – after all, that's what monsters are supposed to do, right? Right!

As we have demonstrated time and time again: just below its face of seemingly pleasant normality, Texas is a seriously strange state, and one that is filled to the absolute brim with a veritable menagerie of fantastic creatures and nightmarish beasts just waiting to surface from their darkened, shadowy lairs and scare the living daylights out of you. And if they have done precisely that, then let us know!

If a giant Mothman-like creature was seen perched precariously upon the roof of your house; if Bigfoot destroyed your car just for daring to look at him; or if your beloved speed-boat was sunk by some monster of the murky depths, then tell us all about it and we'll be there to carry out an investigate of the distinctly weird kind before you can utter the word "Sasquatch!". After all: Volume II of *Monsters of Texas* is already beckoning!

ABOUT THE AUTHORS

Nick Redfern is the author of many books on the world of the paranormal, UFOs, cryptozoology and conspiracy theories, including *Man-Monkey, On the Trail of the Saucer Spies, Science Fiction Secrets, A Covert Agenda, Celebrity Secrets, Body Snatchers in the Desert, Memoirs of a Monster Hunter*, and *There's Something in the Woods*. Nick writes regularly for *UFO Magazine, Fortean Times, Paranormal Magazine, Fate* and many more in-print publications. He also writes a regular, weekly column on cryptozoology, titled *Lair of the Beasts*, for Mania.com. In addition, Nick coordinates much of the work of the U.S. office of the British-based Centre for Fortean Zoology. Nick lists his hobbies as: listening to loud and fast punk-rock music; watching super-violent zombie films; wearing black clothes; reading the works of Jack Kerouac; drinking Carlsberg Special Brew beer; and mystifying Texans with his city of Birmingham, England accent.

Originally from England, he lives with his wife, Dana (who is not a fan of cryptozoology – not at all, in fact), in Arlington, Texas. Nick can be reached at his website: **nickredfern.com**

Ken Gerhard is a cryptozoologist and paranormal researcher whose work and investigations have been featured on several television programs including *Monster Quest, The Real Wolf-man* and *Legend Hunters*. In addition, Ken has authored two previous books about strange creatures: *Big Bird: Modern Sightings of Flying Monsters* and *Monsters are Real!* Born on Friday the 13th, Ken has been fascinated by monsters and mysterious animals since he was a boy. His adventurous mother first dazzled him with stories about weird creatures like Ohio's Mothman, and the Minnesota Iceman. Ultimately, unexplained beasts became Ken's lifelong obsession. A resident of Texas for 31 years, Ken has traveled around the world to 26 different countries, searching for evidence of real monsters. His personal investigations include quests to find Bigfoot-style creatures in North and Central America, Scotland's Loch Ness Monster, werewolves in France and flying humanoids in Mexico. Ken is also an accomplished musician who resides in San Antonio, Texas. He can be reached at his website: **kengerhard.com**

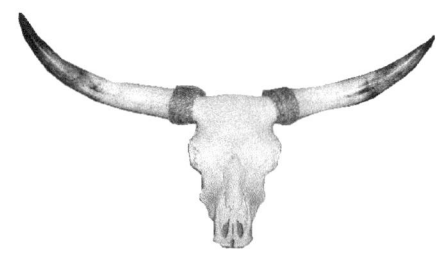

References and Resources

Chapter I: *Big Bird and Other Winged Monsters*
Creatures of the Outer Edge, Jerome Clark and Loren Coleman, Warner Books, 1978
Cessna-Sized Big Birds Swoop over Teachers, K. Mack Sisk, *San Antonio Light*, February 26, 1976
Expert trying to identify mysterious bird flying around Texas, Joe Conger, *KENS5 Eyewitness News*, San Antonio, November 16, 2007
Flying Creature in Texas, www.cryptozoology.com, 2007

Chapter II: *Lone Star Werewolves*
Of Wolves and Men, Barry Lopez, Touchstone Books, 1982
Dallas Morning News, June 2, 1888
Hunting the American Werewolf, Linda Godfrey, Trails Books, 2006
Dallas Morning News, January 29, 1908
Fate, 1960
Weird Texas, Wesley Treat, Heather Shade and Rob Riggs, Sterling Publishing Co., Inc., 2005
Scare-Wolves, Nick Redfern, *Paranormal*, February 2009

Chapter III: *El Chupacabras Comes to Texas*
The Mystery of the Elmendorf Beast, Whitley Strieber's Unknown Country, August 24, 2004
Was it el chupacabra? West Texas man kills chicken slayer, Sidney Levesque, Scripps *Howard News Service*, September 7, 2005
Monster or Dog? 'Goatsucker' Tale Debated, Elizabeth White, *Associated Press*, August 31, 2007
Two "chupacabras" shot, killed in DeWitt County, Victoria Advocate, August 30, 2008

Chapter IV: *The Navidad Wild Man*
www.wildmanofthenavidad.com
Wild Things, Paul Sieveking, *Fortean Times*, No. 161
Of Wolves and Men, Barry Lopez, Touchstone Books, 1982
Wild Woman of the Navidad: www.texasescapes.com
The Legends of Texas, edited by J. Frank Dobie, Texas Folklore Society, 1924
The Wild Woman of the Navidad: www.bigfootencounters.com/creatures/navidad.htm

Chapter V: *Trailing the Texan Bigfoot*
Sasquatch: The Apes Among Us, John Green, Cheam Publishing, 1978
His Face Is Pushed In And His Ears Point, Bill Moore, *El Paso Times*, September 20, 1975
'Big Foot' Terrorizes Kelly Area, San Antonio Light, September 1, 1976
Four Sightings of Hairy Creature Reported in South San Area, Chicano Times, September 3, 1976
Youths Report Attack By the 'Hawley Him', Roger Downing, *Abilene Reporter-News*, July 7, 1977
Slew of 'something' sightings starts Sasquatch Watch, Kathy Jackson, *Dallas Times* and *Dallas Morning News*, February 27, 1992
Horizon City's Monster, Adriana M. Chavez, *El Paso City Times*, July 31, 2003
Is Bigfoot In Texas?, Sheryl Smith-Rodgers, *Country Lifestyle Magazine*, July-August, 2006

Chapter VI: *Big Thicket Beasts*
The Big Thicket Directory of Southeast Texas: www.bigthicketdirectory.com
Big Thicket National Preserve: www.nps.gov/bith
Big Thicket National Preserve:
http://gorpaway.com/gorp/resource/us_national_park//tx_big_t.htm
Handbook of Texas Online: www.tsha.utexas.edu/handbook/online/articles/BB/gkb3.htm
Ghost Road of Hardin County: www.bigthicketdirectory.com
The Bragg Road Ghost Lights: www.qsl.net/w5www/bragg.html
In the Big Thicket, Rob Riggs, Paraview Press, 2001
Bigfoot in Texas? www.texasbigfoot.com/texbfhist1.html
Bragg Road: The Ghost Road of Hardin County, Texas:
www.bigthicketdirectory.com/ghostroad.htm
The Bragg Road Ghost Lights: www.qsl.net/w5www/bragg/html

Chapter VII: *Monsters of the Dark Waters*
Mysterious America (revised edition)*,* Loren Coleman, Paraview Press, 2000
A Gil Blas in California, Alexandre Dumas, Primavera Press, 1993
200-Foot Sea Serpent seen at 3 Bells in Gulf of Mexico, New York Times, July 1, 1908
For the Love of the Lake: www.whiterocklake.org/content/view/130/81/
White Rock Lake Museum: www.whiterocklakemuseum.org/index/htm
White Rock Lake Foundation: www.whiterocklakefoundation.org
50 Reasons to Love (and Save) White Rock Lake, D Magazine, March 1995

Chapter VIII: *Goat Man Terror*

Man or Beast? Goatman Lore Reborn in Fort Worth, Dallas Morning News, October 21, 1999
Fishy Man-Goat Terrifies Couples Parked at Lake Worth, Fort Worth Star-Telegram, July 10, 1969
Memoirs of a Monster Hunter, Nick Redfern, New Page Books, 2005
Weird Texas, Wesley Treat, Heather Shade & Rob Riggs, Sterling Publishing Co., Inc., 2005
Bigfoot in Texas?: www.bigfootproject.org/articles/bf_in_texas.html
For the Love of the Lake: www.whiterocklake.org/content/view/130/81/
White Rock Lake Museum: www.whiterocklakemuseum.org/index/htm
White Rock Lake Foundation: www.whiterocklakefoundation.org
50 Reasons to Love (and Save) White Rock Lake, D Magazine, March 1995

Chapter IX: *Fringe Creatures*

Unexplained Mysteries of the 20th Century, Janet and Colin Bord, Contemporary Books, 1989
When Darkness Falls: Tales of San Antonio Ghosts and Hauntings, Docia Schultz Williams, Republic of Texas Press, 1998
The Mountain Boomer, Jimmy Ward, *Far Out Magazine*, Vol. 1, No. 4, summer 1993
Unearthly Batman Terrifies Watchers, Houston Chronicle, June 19, 1953
El Cucuy has roots deep in border folklore, Kevin Garcia, *Brownsville Herald*, December 31, 2005

Chapter X: *The Horror of Hecate Hill*

www.hecatehill.com and www.levelgroundfilms.com

Chapter XI: *Out-of-place Animals*

Mystery Cats of the World: From Blue Tigers to Exmoor Beasts, Dr. Karl P.N. Shuker, Robert Hale Books, 1989
Are Black Panthers terrorizing Dialville?, Hanna Buchanan, *Jacksonville Progress*, March 22, 2007
Black Panther Sightings in Upshur County, Bob Hallmark, *KLTV*, Longview, TX, March 28, 2007
Black Panthers: Did Such an Animal Ever Exist?, W.T. Bloc, www.wtblock.com, 1998
The Legendary Snow Monkeys of Texas, Ed Baker, *Austin Chronicle*, August 5, 2005
Kangaroo escapes from vet's yard in Lewisville, Emily Tsao, *Dallas Morning News*, December 4, 2007
Wayward Texas manatee released in Florida waters, Associated Press, September 13, 2007

Chapter XII: *Bigfoot – East Texan Style*

The Bigfoot Casebook, Janet and Colin Bord, Stackpole Books, 1982
Boy says for real sighting of monster renews Marion legend, Irvin Power, *Marshall News*

Messenger, September 1, 1965
Killer Creature Stalks Vidor Area, John Rice, *Orange Leader*, June 20, 1978
The Monkey Man of 1409, www.i-dineout.com, Liberty County, TX, June 14, 2003
Tom Slick – True Life Encounters in Cryptozoology, Loren Coleman, Linden Publishing, 2002
The Caddo Lake History Page: www.caddolake.com/history.htm
Caddo Lake, Texas-Louisiana: http://ops.tamu.edu/x075bb/caddo/caddo.html
Caddo Lake Area, Chamber of Commerce and Tourism: History: http://caddolake.org/

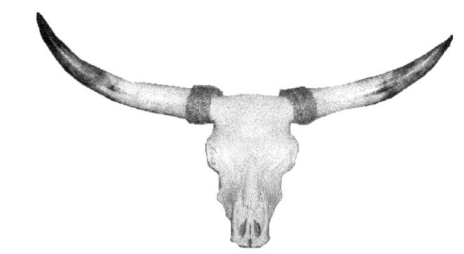

Acknowledgments

We would like to offer our sincere thanks and appreciation to all of those people who were willing to share with us the details of their own, personal encounters with the many and varied unknown animals of Texas – without you, this book could never have been written.

We would also like to offer a very special thank you to the following people: Jonathan Downes (the editor and publisher of this book) and everyone at the Centre for Fortean Zoology; Phylis & Steve Canion, Harvey Hayek & Family, Devin McAnally, Shawn Gregory & Family, Reggie Lagow, Mr. & Mrs. Greg Davis, Maria Cantu, Benjamin & Cris Aum, Blanca Trevino, Deborah Fisher, Frank Ramirez, Jym Evans, Pete Haviland & Lone Star Spirits, Joe Conger & KENS-5, White Wolf Productions, KPI/Lightworks Productions, Storyhouse Productions, CMJ Productions; Rob Riggs; Bill Fountain; Justin Meeks; and Duane Graves.

Naomi West with husband Richie—two of the latest generation of Texas monster hunters

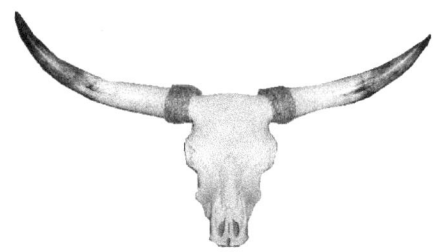

Texas Monster Hunters, Past & Present

Tom Slick

Although he was born in Pennsylvania and raised in Oklahoma, it was while living in Texas, and particularly in his beloved San Antonio, that this high-profile adventurer had his greatest impact. Most old-timers in the Alamo City remember the handsome and dashing oil tycoon, inventor and collector, who founded the well-known Southwest Research Institute, owned his own airstrip and traveled the world hunting and fishing, often in search of hidden treasures and mysterious animals.

Slick came from a family with a famous and colorful background and he was smart, attending Yale, Harvard and M.I.T. Universities while majoring in engineering, the natural sciences and medicine. Tom loved intrigue and exploration. While in college, he made a trek to Scotland, in order to investigate reports of the Loch Ness Monster.

In 1957, after he had made his fortune, Slick organized a pair of expeditions to search for the abominable snowman, or Yeti, of the Himalayas, complete with an official endorsement from the San Antonio Zoo. During the first trip, he was badly hurt in a bus accident, but still succeeded in discovering tracks and other evidence that made him a firm believer.

In 1959, Tom shifted his focus to northern California and backed some of the earliest and most noteworthy Bigfoot expeditions ever undertaken. He also mounted searches for the mysterious, manlike Orang Pendek of Sumatra, as well as giant salamanders in northern California and enormous fish sighted in Alaska's Lake Illiamna. Tragically, Tom Slick died in an airplane crash over Montana in 1962, at the age of 46.

Sallie Ann Clarke

During July of 1969, reports of the Lake Worth Monster began making headlines in Fort Worth, Texas. Several people claimed to have encountered a shaggy, white, goat man, frolicking in the forests of the Greer Island Nature Center, on the outskirts of the city.

Aspiring writer and private investigator Sallie Ann was intrigued by the stories and quickly became a regular, among the curiosity seekers that scoured the woods of Lake Worth on a nightly basis, looking for the creature. Clarke personally interviewed many eyewitnesses and ultimately claimed to have had three, fleeting glimpses of the monster herself.

Her subsequent interest and in-depth research into the phenomena resulted in her only book titled, *The Lake Worth Monster: Of Greer Island, Ft. Worth, Texas*. Admittedly, Clarke incorporated elements of fiction into her book in order to make it more entertaining to readers, but later regretted doing so following her own encounters. After her book's publication, Sallie Ann continued to collect reports of the monster. Sallie Ann Clarke passed away recently, on November 03, 2009.

Jimmy Chilcutt

Formerly a forensic fingerprint expert for the Conroe, Texas police department, Chilcutt has discovered some of the most compelling evidence in support of the existence of Bigfoot. He has authenticated so-called dermatoglyphics or skin ridges, which seem to be visible on a handful of Bigfoot track casts.

Jimmy's interest in non-human primates began in 1995, when it occurred to him that he could learn a great deal about human prints by studying those of apes and monkeys. He arranged to study, and fingerprint, a thousand or so different primates from various collections around the United States. One evening, Chilcutt was watching a television documentary about Bigfoot and decided that he could use his unique expertise in order to debunk the dermal ridges that were, alleged to be visible in plaster casts of their tracks. However, after studying several casts in the collection of physical anthropologist Dr. Jeff Meldrum, Jimmy was amazed by what he found.

Five different Bigfoot tracks from different locations seemed to contain ridges belonging to an unknown primate species. The ridges were much thicker than those of a human and flowed in a different direction to that of any known primate. Chilcutt also found evidence of natural scarring in some of the ridges. He concluded that some Bigfoot tracks must indeed belong to an unknown species of primate roaming the woods of North America.

Chester Moore, Jr.

Born and raised amidst the piney woods of east Texas, Moore is a noted outdoorsman, conservationist and adventurer, and has written for many of the top sporting magazines in Texas. In addition, he has appeared on television, radio and in a several outdoor videos. As a child, Moore – known as the Cryptokeeper – was heavily influenced by the movie, *The Legend of*

Boggy Creek and also by unexplained experiences he had while hunting with his father, in the bottoms of Newton and Orange Counties.

After getting his degree in zoology, Chester began to search for evidence of Bigfoot creatures in south-east Texas, which resulted in his writing two books on the subject, *Bigfoot South* and *Bigfoot Lives – Deal With It!*

He has also investigated sightings of Bigfoot in northern California, and has searched for the Ivory-Billed Woodpecker in Arkansas and Red Wolves in Texas. His international expeditions have included visits to Venezuela, where he sought out giant snakes and Spain, where he pursued giant catfish and big cats. In addition to his other activities, Chester is the lead-singer for the metal band *Freak 13*, as well as being a horror movie enthusiast.

For more information, see: **http://www.projectzooquest.com**

Paul Nation

Paul is an investigator of reports of living pterosaurs and comes from Granbury, Texas. He has undertaken four, different expeditions to Papua New Guinea, searching for a winged monster known as the Ropen.

With a total of over 16 weeks spent in the rain forests of New Guinea, Paul ranks as the top Ropen researcher in the world. He became involved in the search for living pterosaurs, due to his background with handling large ratites: flightless birds like ostriches and emus.

His expedition in late 2006 resulted in many night time sightings and Nation even managed to videotape two peculiar lights in the sky from a ridge above one of his camps. This is important because many eyewitnesses have claimed that the Ropen emits a strange bioluminescent glow at night.

The video footage was, analyzed by a missile defense physicist who verified that the two light sources were not created by fakery, camera artifacts, meteors, airplanes, auto headlights, or lanterns.

Paul's most recent expedition turned up more pterosaur reports, but no sightings. Paul is currently making plans to return to Papua New Guinea and to continue his research in an extremely remote area where he has heard that Ropens are more common.

For more information, see. **sites.google.com/site/paulnationexplorer**

Bobby Hamilton

The founder and head of the Gulf Coast Bigfoot Research Organization, Bobby had a traumatic encounter with one of the monsters while growing up as a boy in the small eastern town of Garrison, Texas.

On one particular night, he was startled by an enormous, ape-faced creature peering in the window of his family's remote, rural home. The being appeared to be motioning to Bobby with its finger, as if to draw the boy outside. Hamilton never spoke to anyone about his experience, until years later when he confided in his two older brothers, who confessed that they too seen the Bigfoot peering in their window on different occasions. In addition, some of the family's livestock had been killed by an unknown predator. On at least one occasion, they had heard strange, guttural noises coming from their barn.

The experiences had a profound impact on Hamilton, who made it his life's mission to hunt these elusive hominids, which has resulted in some scary encounters. Subsequently, he has investigated reports of Bigfoot all over east Texas.

Bobby once admitted to me that his passion to prove Bigfoot's existence is so intense, that he surrounds himself with large-caliber weapons and state-of-the-art night vision technology. Hamilton and his group feel that only a Bigfoot's remains will provide sufficient proof of the creature's existence.

Bobby spent some time as a professional wrestler during the 1980s, appearing frequently on television.

For more information, see: **Gulf Coast Bigfoot Research Organization – http:// www.gcbro.com**

Rob Riggs

Rob Riggs is the author of the 2001 book *In the Big Thicket: On the Trail of the Wildman*, published by Paraview Press. Rob is a journalist and the former publisher of a series of award-winning community newspapers in Texas. His interest in "ghost lights," "wild man" sightings and related phenomena began as a child when he heard tales about them in his hometown of Sour Lake in Big Thicket country.

Riggs began writing about the subject more than 20 years ago while working as a reporter for the *Kountze News*. Since then, his studies of the phenomenon have been featured in the *Houston Chronicle* and the *Beaumont Enterprise*.

Rob has also consulted on ghost lights for Waseda University in Tokyo and the Harvard College Observatory.

For more information, see: **http://www.paraview.com/riggs/index.htm**

The Texas Bigfoot Research Conservancy

The TBRC is a non-profit, scientific research organization that is comprised of dozens of volunteer investigators, naturalists and scientists. The group had its origins in May 1994, when Craig Woolheater and his fiancé saw a large, hairy, man-like beast while driving at night on a highway between New Orleans and Alexandria, Louisiana.

With a diverse and dedicated roster, the TBRC pursues education and research activities relative to the centuries-old reports of "wild men" in the United States, and holds a yearly conference in the town of Tyler, Texas.

The TBRC proposes that the source of the Bigfoot phenomenon is a biological entity, probably an "unlisted large primate."

For more information, see: **www.texasbigfoot.org**

Naomi West

Naomi West says: "I was born and raised in West Virginia, daughter of a minister. I was always looking for adventures and unexplained mysteries as a kid, and my first area of paranormal interest was the topic of the Biblical Nephilim.

"I have always loved animals – everything from whales to bugs – with pet rats being the dearest to my heart. I am a performing soloist, but writing is my true passion. I live in Central Texas and currently teach high school English, but I hope to be a full time writer someday.

"My husband tests weapons systems for the military here at Ft. Hood, and he is also a musician and fellow UFO enthusiast. We are both MUFON field investigators.

"Since my involvement with CFZ, I have discovered that Central Texas has contributed most recently with the blue dog sightings, where my interest currently lies. I will always be most fascinated with the Loch Ness monster. Fortean Zoology combines my love of mystery with love for animals.

"Being a woman in a masculine oriented world has never been an issue for me; rather, I resent being a woman in a world where both genders, at social functions, continually try to separate into 'gender-oriented' activities: I don't cook, I hate shopping, I dislike 'chick flicks', I have never had kids, I love theology and science fiction... oh yes, and did I mention pet rats?

"More difficult than being a woman is being a student of the paranormal in Christian circles as well as an Orthodox Christian in paranormal circles, or, for that matter, an animal lover amid hunters, or a meat-eater amid Vegans.

"I love people from most all schools of thought, but find myself often a member of opposing groups and always worried one group will throw me out when they learn I am not necessarily on their bandwagon. But I have received grace from all groups around me – from pagans to atheists to Christians to people who think our government leaders are all Reptilians, and in the end, I just love people... almost as much as animals."

For more information see **http://westruth.blogspot.com/**

THE CENTRE FOR FORTEAN ZOOLOGY

So, what is the Centre for Fortean Zoology?

We are a non profit-making organisation founded in 1992 with the aim of being a clearing house for information, and coordinating research into mystery animals around the world. We also study out of place animals, rare and aberrant animal behaviour, and Zooform Phenomena; little-understood "things" that appear to be animals, but which are in fact nothing of the sort, and not even alive (at least in the way we understand the term).

Why should I join the Centre for Fortean Zoology?

Not only are we the biggest organisation of our type in the world, but - or so we like to think - we are the best. We are certainly the only truly global Cryptozoological research organisation, and we carry out our investigations using a strictly scientific set of guidelines. We are expanding all the time and looking to recruit new members to help us in our research into mysterious animals and strange creatures across the globe. Why should you join us? Because, if you are genuinely interested in trying to solve the last great mysteries of Mother Nature, there is nobody better than us with whom to do it.

What do I get if I join the Centre for Fortean Zoology?

For £12 a year, you get a four-issue subscription to our journal *Animals & Men*. Each issue contains 60 pages packed with news, articles, letters, research papers, field reports, and even a gossip column! The magazine is A5 in format with a full colour cover. You also have access to one of the world's largest collections of resource material dealing with cryptozoology and allied disciplines, and people from the CFZ membership regularly take part in fieldwork and expeditions around the world.

How is the Centre for Fortean Zoology organised?

The CFZ is managed by a three-man board of trustees, with a non-profit making trust registered with HM Government Stamp Office. The board of trustees is supported by a Permanent Directorate of full and part-time staff, and advised by a Consultancy Board of specialists - many of whom are world-renowned experts in their particular field. We have regional representatives across the UK, the USA, and many other parts of the world, and are affiliated with other organisations whose aims and protocols mirror our own.

I am new to the subject, and although I am interested I have little practical knowledge. I don't want to feel out of my depth. What should I do?

Don't worry. We were *all* beginners once. You'll find that the people at the CFZ are friendly and approachable. We have a thriving forum on the website which is the hub of an ever-growing electronic community. You will soon find your feet. Many members of the CFZ Permanent Directorate started off as ordinary members, and now work full-time chasing monsters around the world.

I have an idea for a project which isn't on your website. What do I do?

Write to us, e-mail us, or telephone us. The list of future projects on the website is not exhaustive. If you have a good idea for an investigation, please tell us. We may well be able to help.

How do I go on an expedition?

We are always looking for volunteers to join us. If you see a project that interests you, do not hesitate to get in touch with us. Under certain circumstances we can help provide funding for your trip. If you look on the future projects section of the website, you can see some of the projects that we have pencilled in for the next few years.

In 2003 and 2004 we sent three-man expeditions to Sumatra looking for Orang-Pendek - a semi-legendary bipedal ape. The same three went to Mongolia in 2005. All three members started off merely subscribers to the CFZ magazine.

Next time it could be you!

Project Kerinci, Sumatra - 2003
In search of the bipedal ape Orang Pendek

How is the Centre for Fortean Zoology funded?

We have no magic sources of income. All our funds come from donations, membership fees, works that we do for TV, radio or magazines, and sales of our publications and merchandise. We are always looking for corporate sponsorship, and other sources of revenue. If you have any ideas for fund-raising please let us know. However, unlike other cryptozoological organisations in the past, we do not live in an intellectual ivory tower. We are not afraid to get our hands dirty, and furthermore we are not one of those organisations where the membership have to raise money so that a privileged few can go on expensive foreign trips. Our research teams, both in the UK and abroad, consist of a mixture of experienced and inexperienced personnel. We are truly a community, and work on the premise that the benefits of CFZ membership are open to all.

What do you do with the data you gather from your investigations and expeditions?

Reports of our investigations are published on our website as soon as they are available. Preliminary reports are posted within days of the project finishing.

Each year we publish a 200 page yearbook containing research papers and expedition reports too long to be printed in the journal. We freely circulate our information to anybody who asks for it.

No. Each year since 2000 we have held our annual convention - the *Weird Weekend* - in Exeter. It is three days of lectures, workshops, and excursions. But most importantly it is a chance for members of the CFZ to meet each other, and to talk with the members of the permanent directorate in a relaxed and informal setting and preferably with a pint of beer in one hand. Since 2006 - the *Weird Weekend* has been bigger and better and held on the third weekend in August in the idyllic rural location of Woolsery in North Devon.

Since relocating to North Devon in 2005 we have become ever more closely involved with other community organisations, and we hope that this trend will continue. We also work closely with Police Forces across the UK as consultants for animal mutilation cases, and we intend to forge closer links with the coastguard and other community services. We want to work closely with those who regularly travel into the Bristol Channel, so that if the recent trend of exotic animal visitors to our coastal waters continues, we can be out there as soon as possible.

We are building a Visitor's Centre in rural North Devon. This will not be open to the general public, but will provide a museum, a library and an educational resource for our members (currently over 400) across the globe. We are also planning a youth organisation which will involve children and young people in our activities.

Apart from having been the only Fortean Zoological organisation in the world to have consistently published material on all aspects of the subject for over a decade, we have achieved the following concrete results:

- Disproved the myth relating to the headless so-called sea-serpent carcass of Durgan beach in Cornwall 1975
- Disproved the story of the 1988 puma skull of Lustleigh Cleave
- Carried out the only in-depth research ever into the mythos of the Cornish Owlman
- Made the first records of a tropical species of lamprey
- Made the first records of a luminous cave gnat larva in Thailand
- Discovered a possible new species of British mammal - the beech marten
- In 1994-6 carried out the first archival fortean zoological survey of Hong Kong
- In the year 2000, CFZ theories were confirmed when an new species of lizard was added to the British list
- Identified the monster of Martin Mere in Lancashire as a giant wels catfish
- Expanded the known range of Armitage's skink in the Gambia by 80%
- Obtained photographic evidence of the remains of Europe's largest known pike
- Carried out the first ever in-depth study of the *ninki-nanka*
- Carried out the first attempt to breed Puerto Rican cave snails in captivity
- Were the first European explorers to visit the `lost valley` in Sumatra
- Published the first ever evidence for a new tribe of pygmies in Guyana
- Published the first evidence for a new species of caiman in Guyana
- Filmed unknown creatures on a monster-haunted lake in Ireland for the first time
- Had a sighting of orang pendek in Sumatra in 2009
- Published some of the best evidence ever for the almasty in southern Russia

EXPEDITIONS & INVESTIGATIONS TO DATE INCLUDE:

- 1998 Puerto Rico, Florida, Mexico *(Chupacabras)*
- 1999 Nevada *(Bigfoot)*
- 2000 Thailand *(Giant snakes called nagas)*
- 2002 Martin Mere *(Giant catfish)*
- 2002 Cleveland *(Wallaby mutilation)*
- 2003 Bolam Lake *(BHM Reports)*
- 2003 Sumatra *(Orang Pendek)*
- 2003 Texas *(Bigfoot; giant snapping turtles)*
- 2004 Sumatra *(Orang Pendek; cigau, a sa-bre-toothed cat)*
- 2004 Illinois *(Black panthers; cicada swarm)*
- 2004 Texas *(Mystery blue dog)*
- Loch Morar *(Monster)*
- 2004 Puerto Rico *(Chupacabras; carnivorous cave snails)*
- 2005 Belize *(Affiliate expedition for hairy dwarfs)*
- 2005 Loch Ness *(Monster)*
- 2005 Mongolia *(Allghoi Khorkhoi aka Mongolian death worm)*
- 2006 Gambia *(Gambian sea monster , Ninki Nanka and Armitage's skink*
- 2006 Llangorse Lake *(Giant pike, giant eels)*
- 2006 Windermere *(Giant eels)*
- 2007 Coniston Water *(Giant eels)*
- 2007 Guyana *(Giant anaconda, didi, water tiger)*
- 2008 Russia *(Almasty)*
- 2009 Sumatra *(Orang pendek)*
- 2009 Republic of Ireland *(Lake Monster)*
- 2010 Texas *(Blue dogs)*

Other books available from
CFZ PRESS

CFZ PRESS

ONLY FOOLS AND GOATSUCKERS
Jonathan Downes - ISBN 0-9512872-3-0

£12.50

In January and February 1998 Jonathan Downes and Graham Inglis of the Centre for Fortean Zoology spent three and a half weeks in Puerto Rico, Mexico and Florida, accompanied by a film crew from UK Channel 4 TV. Their aim was to make a documentary about the terrifying chupacabra - a vampiric creature that exists somewhere in the grey area between folklore and reality. This remarkable book tells the gripping, sometimes scary, and often hilariously funny story of how the boys from the CFZ did their best to subvert the medium of contemporary TV documentary making and actually do their job.

WHILE THE CAT'S AWAY
Chris Moiser - ISBN: 0-9512872-1-4

£7.99

Over the past thirty years or so there have been numerous sightings of large exotic cats, including black leopards, pumas and lynx, in the South West of England. Former Rhodesian soldier Sam McCall moved to North Devon and became a farmer and pub owner when Rhodesia became Zimbabwe in 1980. Over the years despite many of his pub regulars having seen the "Beast of Exmoor" Sam wasn't at all sure that it existed. Then a series of happenings made him change his mind. Chris Moiser—a zoologist—is well known for his research into the mystery cats of the westcountry. This is his first novel.

CFZ EXPEDITION REPORT 2006 - GAMBIA
ISBN 1905723032

£12.50

In July 2006, The J.T.Downes memorial Gambia Expedition - a six-person team - Chris Moiser, Richard Freeman, Chris Clarke, Oll Lewis, Lisa Dowley and Suzi Marsh went to the Gambia, West Africa. They went in search of a dragon-like creature, known to the natives as `Ninki Nanka`, which has terrorized the tiny African state for generations, and has reportedly killed people as recently as the 1990s. They also went to dig up part of a beach where an amateur naturalist claims to have buried the carcass of a mysterious fifteen foot sea monster named 'Gambo', and they sought to find the Armitage's Skink (*Chalcides armitagei*) - a tiny lizard first described in 1922 and only rediscovered in 1989. Here, for the first time, is their story.... With an forward by Dr. Karl Shuker and introduction by Jonathan Downes.

BIG CATS IN BRITAIN YEARBOOK 2006
Edited by Mark Fraser - ISBN 978-1905723-01-0

£10.00

Big cats are said to roam the British Isles and Ireland even now as you are sitting and reading this. People from all walks of life encounter these mysterious felines on a daily basis in every nook and cranny of these two countries. Most are jet-black, some are white, some are brown, in fact big cats of every description and colour are seen by some unsuspecting person while on his or her daily business. 'Big Cats in Britain' are the largest and most active group in the British Isles and Ireland This is their first book. It contains a run-down of every known big cat sighting in the UK during 2005, together with essays by various luminaries of the British big cat research community which place the phenomenon into scientific, cultural, and historical perspective.

**CFZ PRESS, MYRTLE COTTAGE,
WOOLSERY, BIDEFORD,
NORTH DEVON, EX39 5QR
w w w . c f z . o r g . u k**

Other books available from
CFZ PRESS

CFZ PRESS

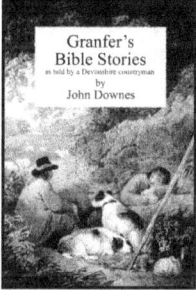

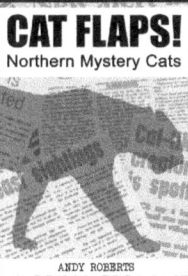

Other books available from
CFZ PRESS

www.ingramcontent.com/pod-product-compliance
Lightning Source LLC
Chambersburg PA
CBHW050658290626
47170CB00015B/1946